"You'd better watch it. You'll get more than you bargained for with that, little lady," Celia said nervously.

"Maybe I want more," Maggie said and kissed her again.

Celia's resistance and caution suddenly became things of the past. She succumbed to all she was feeling. If it meant punishment and remorse tomorrow then so be it, but right now she wanted that woman. Celia buried her face in Maggie's breasts. Tears formed, and she tasted the salt mingled with Maggie's soft brown nipples. Touch, taste, smell enveloped Celia until she was totally lost in Maggie's body.

# SAXON BENNETT

THE NAIAD PRESS, INC.
1996

Printed in the United States of America on acid-free paper
First Edition

Editor: Lisa Epson
Cover designer: Bonnie Liss (Phoenix Graphics)
Typesetter: Sandi Stancil


**Library of Congress Cataloging-in-Publication Data**

Bennett, Saxon. 1961 –
     The wish list / by Saxon Bennett.
          p.        cm.
     ISBN 1-56280-125-2 (alk. paper)
     1. Lesbians—Fiction.    I. Title.
PS3552.E547544W57    1996
813'.54—dc20                                                    95-25875
                                                                        CIP

# Dedication

My eternal gratitude to Lin for plucking me from the morass of my own egotism, for reminding me of the virtues of having fun, and for all the lovely hours spent in your arms. For the furry friend in my life Sir J. H. Crapapore, what would I do without you to sit on my manuscript and type all those zzzz on the keyboard with your tail. I love you both.

## About the Author

My wife tells me I'm only interested in five things: reading, writing, biking, fucking, and gardening, not necessarily in that order. At first I was appalled at being so easily categorized, but you know, she's right. There's not much more to me.

I have a B.A. in English from the University of Minnesota. I live in Phoenix, Arizona, because I love saguaro cactus and the desert. The life of a simple minded soul in perpetual need of a drink of water, that's me.

# Chapter One

Amanda stood behind the tiled island in the center of the kitchen, waiting for her toast to pop up and talking to her mother, who was not paying attention to her. Maggie was intently watching the swirls of cream in her coffee as she stirred them into the brown liquid.

"Mom, are you listening to me?" Amanda asked.

Maggie looked up; her green-gray eyes had that faraway look that Amanda disliked.

"Yes, I am listening, Amanda," Maggie replied, lying without hesitation. Amanda was like Harold, always demanding her attention. Maggie had grown used to the reprimands. She would smile as they rolled their eyes in exasperation. Harold and Amanda thought she was flighty. It was more like bored. Maggie went for mind-walks when she was bored or troubled. She was thinking of the ticket and Celia's note when Amanda caught her wandering.

"Then what was I saying?" Amanda demanded.

"Would you like a summary or would you prefer verbatim?"

"I know you weren't listening. Why don't you just admit it?"

"All right, I wasn't listening. I'm listening now. Please tell me again what you were saying."

"No, you tell me what you're thinking about."

Maggie studied Amanda's features. They were a strange fusion of hers and Harold's. This other human being had been created out of something as simple as lust. Amanda was twenty-five. She had her father's brown eyes and his furrowed forehead. She had her mother's nose and mouth and luckily, since Harold had ended up being a rather stout figure. Amanda had her mother's lithe body combined with her father's dark good looks. She was purposeful and opinionated and, for such a young woman, had a possessive, dominating manner.

"I was thinking about an old friend of mine."

"Who is that?"

"Her name is Celia. I might go visit her in Arizona."

"How come I've never heard about her before?"

"There wasn't really any need."

"Mom, save us both time. Who is she really and why has she been a secret up until now?"

"She was engaged to your father when they were in college."

"What happened? Why would you go visit her now?"

"She was my best friend. It's a long, complicated story, Amanda. I don't think you'd understand."

"Try me."

Maggie looked at her daughter and felt the nagging need to confide a long-buried memory. Amanda, by virtue of timing and nothing more, fulfilled the need.

"Celia and your father were engaged. Celia fell in love with someone else, and your father had the bad luck to find them together. It was very hard on him."

"That wasn't very decent of Celia to play around on her fiancé. She should have broken it off first."

"We all think that, Amanda, but sometimes it isn't that easy. Things happen, and they are not always neat and well-timed."

"Is that why you never talked about her? Because she dumped Dad and you married him instead?"

"It's part of it. Your father and I were always close friends. After Celia left, things just took their course."

"So Dad was rebounding when you picked him up. You weren't the one great passion of his life."

"Amanda, that's not fair. Your father and I loved each other very much. We were better suited for each other."

"So what was he like?"

"Who?"

"The man Dad got dumped for."

"Amanda, I don't want to talk about this any

3

more. I'm tired now. I think I'll go lie down. I'll call you tomorrow."

"I don't understand why you want to visit a woman who hurt Dad like that."

"Neither do I, exactly."

Amanda looked at her mother and furrowed her brow. "All right, I'll talk to you tomorrow."

Maggie lay down, running her hand across the indentation of Harold's side of the bed. Amanda's questions kept playing themselves through her head. Why hadn't she told Amanda the truth? Was it because Celia had left Harold for another woman? If it had been a man would she have told Amanda about it? It was harder for everyone that Celia fell in love with Bridgette. Harder still that she packed up and left without so much as a word.

Celia was like that though, a bridge burner. When it was done it was done. So why did she want Maggie to come? Hadn't it been awful enough? Maggie couldn't stop her mind from wandering back to the day she found out.


Sally, Celia's mother, had opened the front door, telling her that Celia was downstairs in her room. "Just go on down honey," Sally said. Maggie had since thought of those words as a portent. Why couldn't Sally have called to Celia, telling her Maggie had come? Celia would have been warned and Maggie spared. But no, things never go the way they should. Harold had called her a pessimist, but Maggie thought herself a pragmatist who firmly subscribed to Murphy's Law: If it could go wrong, it did.

Maggie heard Celia talking to someone. She hadn't meant to eavesdrop. She wished she hadn't. Celia's voice was different, full of an intensity Maggie didn't know.

"But I do love you. I want to be with you. Honest I do. I just need more time. Please. I'll get things straightened around, I promise."

Maggie assumed she was talking to Harold. Funny that Sally hadn't told her that he was there. Maggie was about to knock on the door, when she came face-to-face with Bridgette rushing from the room in tears.

Celia called out after her, "Wait!"

"I can't."

Maggie's confusion was apparent. Celia glanced at her and ran after Bridgette, leaving Maggie to sort out what she had just seen. In the light spring rain, Maggie walked home down by the river. She sat and watched the barges and the rowing skiffs go by, trying to figure out how she felt. Later that night Celia called, but Maggie was already in bed, chilled and sick. For days Maggie avoided Celia, but then Sally called to ask her to come over.

Maggie knew Celia wouldn't be home so she went. She didn't know why. Perhaps it was to make what she was feeling real. Sally confirmed her doubts and now her worst fears. Sally showed her a note she had written to Celia asking her why she spent so many nights away from home and why she was staying with Bridgette and was there something unusual about their friendship and perhaps they should spend a little less time together because it wasn't normal. Celia had written her response on the bottom of the note, saying that Sally wouldn't understand and that Celia couldn't really explain it except to say that she wanted to be with Bridgette and nothing was going to come between them.

"What do you suppose it means?" Sally asked.

"I don't know, and I don't want to know," Maggie replied.

As Maggie left Celia's house, she looked back at the pristine pillars, thinking about the times she and Celia had sat on the front porch and talked. It would never be like that again. Maggie could not decide if she was disgusted or curious or jealous. Maybe she felt all three emotions. Why had Celia chosen Bridgette? Why not Maggie if she liked girls? Had Celia had feelings like that for Maggie? Maggie knew she loved Celia, but lust?

She remembered wishing as they both lay naked in their twin beds, talking in the dark, that one of them was a man so they could always be together, not separated by boyfriends and later husbands. But it hadn't occurred to her that they could be lovers.

Maggie walked to Diva's for beer. It was happy hour. After enough beers anyone could be happy. She was methodically peeling the label on her beer bottle when Harold saw her. He seemed surprised to see her there by herself. He had come with his friend Phil.

"Are you okay?" he asked.

Maggie looked at him and swallowed hard, telling herself not to cry. "Yes, I just had a rough day at school. I thought I'd treat myself."

"Where's Celia? You can usually entice her for a quick cocktail."

"I just stopped by on a whim. In fact, I'd better go."

"No, don't. Stay and have one more with me. I'll buy."

Maggie looked uncertain, but Harold ordered her a beer and she found herself not wanting to go after all. She got slowly drunk and listened to Harold and Phil tell her horror stories about med school. She kept looking at Harold and feeling guilty for knowing things she shouldn't.

She felt like screaming at him, your fiancée is in the arms of another woman and has no intention of marrying you. It's all a farce, Harold. It's never going to happen. Every second that we sit here she gets farther away and there is nothing either of us can do to stop it. But then again, maybe the whole thing will just go away. Maybe if we just keep our mouths shut, Celia can have her little fling. She'll realize that it won't work. It could happen. She took another swig of beer and began to feel better.

"Celia's going to move in with Bridgette," Harold said rather matter-of-factly.

"She is?" Maggie said, stunned.

"Yes, I think it's a good idea."

"Why?"

"I like Bridgette. She's organized and responsible, and I think she'll be a good influence on Celia. Besides, it is time Celia learned what it's like to be out in the world."

"She will make better wife material that way," Maggie replied.

"Crudely put, but yes. I know she's young, but she is flighty."

Maggie ordered another beer. Getting drunk seemed the only thing to do. It might bury the anger she felt welling up. Moving in. Oh, Harold, if you only knew what this means. That responsible woman is fucking your girlfriend, not training her to be your wife. Part of Maggie wanted to crush his bubble, swat it to the ground, but the other part felt an indescribable pity, knowing the hurt she was feeling would be so much more for him.

Maggie rolled over on the bed, unable to sleep, able only to keep remembering those days when everything was falling apart. She watched the snow fall. It was probably warm in Arizona. What did Celia look like now? It was so long ago.

When they had sat on the litter-strewn shore of the Mississippi River, the buds had just begun to bloom. It was Maggie's favorite time of year. The lingering cold was gone. Summer was coming, but Celia was making plans that no longer included her. They walked in silence until they came to the shore.

"Harold told me that you know about me moving in with Bridgette. That wasn't how I wanted you to find out. I wanted to tell you, but you kept avoiding me. I don't really expect you to understand, but I don't want you to hate me. Please don't hate me."

Maggie sat studying her cuticles. "I don't hate

you, and I want to understand. It's just all so strange. Why this? Why now? Are you two sleeping together? What does it all mean, Celia?"

"I'm not really sure. I know that I've never felt this way before. She makes me feel things I didn't think I possessed. I know that I love her. I don't know how things will turn out, but loving women is a part of me that won't go away."

"What are you going to do?"

"Most likely burn a lot of bridges, but I've never been afraid of that. You know me," Celia said, smiling at her.

"This is serious, Celia. You're playing with other people's lives here."

Celia stood up and walked to the water's edge. She turned and looked at Maggie. "Don't you think I know that? Do you think this is easy for me? Loving Bridgette means everything to me, but it doesn't mean I'm certain about anything. Once I jump, there is no going back. Once I say yes, I sleep with women, my whole frame of reference changes. There is no support, no long-standing rules to go by. My mother is ready to commit me to some kind of treatment, and even you, my best friend, act different. Can't you see this is hard for me?"

"And it's easy for the rest of us?" Maggie replied.

Celia looked back out onto the river. "No, I know it's not easy for anyone."

"I feel that I'm losing you, and it hurts. I know people change, but I always thought that we wouldn't, that we would always be there for each other. Now I'm not so sure. I'm not sure of anything anymore."

Maggie couldn't bring herself to mention Harold.

This wasn't about him. This was about loving your best friend and losing her. How could she say now that she wanted to be like Bridgette in Celia's eyes? That she had thoughts but didn't know what to do with them? Celia was right. There wasn't a road map for this.

Maggie got up. She went to the kitchen and opened a long-neck beer. When Harold was alive she had weaned herself of beer because it wasn't a socially acceptable beverage for women. So she had taken to other alcohols. But now she drank beer again.

She knew she had left Celia hurting on the bank of the river that day, but Maggie was hurting too. She left telling Celia not to pull a Virginia Woolf, walking into the river with rocks in her pockets and drowning herself.

Celia managed a smile and said, "It's not like that."

Bravado until the end, Maggie thought bitterly.

Later, things called for true bravery, and Celia managed it. She did have the courage to stand up to everyone. Things got ugly, and Maggie ended up standing on the side of the moral majority. She let Celia down. But it got so complicated. It was awful, that night when Harold discovered them together. Celia should have told him, got it over with instead of waiting, instead of letting him find them like that.

When Maggie answered the phone she could barely understand the sobbing voice on the other end. Finally, she asked, impatient with concern, "Where are you? I'll come get you."

She picked him up and they drove to the bluff that overlooked the city. Night followed twilight, and as the lights below began to flicker, Maggie listened to his story and tried to imagine what he had seen. She held his head in her lap, trying to soothe him. She knew nothing would take away the hurt or disgrace he was feeling. He kept asking over and over again what he had done to make this happen.

Maggie met Celia at her apartment. It was the first time she had been there. It was tastefully, if sparsely, furnished. Bridgette had obvious tastes, and the place reflected them. Maggie was jealous. Why couldn't she be as decisive? Maybe that was why Celia was attracted to Bridgette. Maybe Maggie's wishy-washy ways didn't appeal, but Maggie was still that way. Having tastes, likes, and dislikes meant standing up for yourself. It meant knowing your own mind, and Maggie didn't.

She was angry with Celia that day. Why hadn't she told him? Did she know what she had done to him? How hurt he was? Celia was unwilling to sacrifice her own happiness, her sense of what was right for her life to anyone, much less someone as extraneous as Harold.

"That's what he is to you, extraneous?" Maggie asked.

"To be perfectly honest, yes. He cornered me, and I know that now. My whole life up to now has been a charade. Well, the game's over."

"And am I part of that charade, too?"

"No. You were one of the only real parts. With you I could be myself. With Harold I didn't feel that way."

"I love you, Celia," Maggie blurted.

"I love you, too," Celia said.

They held each other, and as Maggie pulled away she looked deep into Celia's eyes.

"Promise me you'll never forget what we had," Maggie said, and then she kissed Celia on the lips, a lingering kiss that she hoped said all that words could not. Maggie never forgot that kiss. Sometimes she would allow herself to daydream about it, but as the years went by she forced herself to put it away.

When Celia and Bridgette left, Maggie and Harold began spending time together. Both missed Celia, both were envious of Bridgette, and both felt that they were wronged by a woman who had once seemed so harmless. They became lovers, then husband and wife. They bought a house. Maggie, under Harold's careful supervision, landscaped the yard, refinished antiques, and had a child. They lived life like so many before them, and they never spoke of Celia. Now, it seemed so long ago, so far away, it almost wasn't real.

# Chapter Two

The plane left the runway. It was too late to change her mind.

She'd done so a half-dozen times, dragging her luggage up from the cellar to the second story and put it back again. She had pulled clothes from the closet, sorted through them, and put them back; pulled them out, put them back. She had made a pro list and a con list, several lists in fact, with the reasons becoming more abstract and absurd with each one. She had scrunched them up into balls and pitched them across the room.

The day of departure she got up and packed. She didn't think; she did things automatically. She haphazardly flung clothes in two large suitcases. Harold would have been horrified. She called Amanda and left a message on her answering machine. The coward's way out. She took a cab to the airport. In three hours she would be there. She would see Celia.

As the plane passed over the patchwork earth below, Maggie felt apprehension growing like a cold knot in the pit of her stomach. She ordered a martini and thought about Celia. What would she be like? Had it been a good twenty years or a slow hell? What will she think of me?

Maggie suddenly felt conservative, well-mannered, nondescript. A doctor's wife. That was, after all, her lifelong achievement. What was Celia's? What am I doing? What is this jaunting out into the unknown about? Is this some form of midlife crisis? Maybe Amanda wasn't so farfetched thinking that her mother was losing her marbles. But Maggie couldn't tolerate having Amanda shove one more magazine article on older women's various psychoses in her face.

The plane descended. Maggie was scared — there was no turning back. She would have to face whatever was ahead. Seven days. She could put on a brave face for that long. After all, she'd managed that for twenty years.

Celia stood waiting. Her long, curly locks of twenty years ago cut short, nearly shaved at the side and back with a surprising long lock of curls that ran nearly to her waist. She was nut-brown and wore sandals. The easy nature of her denim dress and white shirt told of mannerisms Maggie once knew. Celia put her hand to Maggie's cheek and drew her near. Maggie smelled the sun in her hair, the light scent of perfume and sweat on her neck.

"Thank you so much for coming. I wasn't sure you would," Celia whispered in her ear.

Maggie looked at her and smiled. "I wasn't sure myself until this morning."

"Spontaneity at our age is a good thing, Maggie," Celia replied, taking her arm and leading in the direction of the baggage carousel.

"You're still the only one who brings it out in me."

"We have a week to see just how stodgy you've become."

"You'd be surprised."

Maggie felt the rush of warm air as they left Sky Harbor Airport. She was glad she had the foresight not to wear a sweater.

She watched Celia's tanned arm shift the Jeep as they lurched and weaved through traffic, leaving the skyscrapers of Phoenix behind as they headed toward the unknown horizon.

"What's it like never having winter?"

"Odd at first. There is no sense of death or of renewal. Living here is like an endless vacation. I'm not sure that's good, but it helps stave off depression. It's hard to brood on a beautiful sunny day."

Maggie looked at Celia. Celia had forgotten the

piercing gaze of those green eyes. She quickly looked away.

Maggie broke the silence. "Why now?"

Celia was puzzled for a moment. "Why did I want you to come?"

"Yes."

"You couldn't have come, wouldn't have come, if Harold was alive. I couldn't have asked. Even in those moments when I needed you most, I knew that what happened between the three of us hurt too much. There was no going back."

"You needed me?"

Celia looked at her and squeezed her hand. "More than you'll ever know."

Maggie sat back in her seat and felt a flood of contentment. Celia had thought of her in those years. She was glad she had come.

"So how did you end up here?"

"I came out to finish school, fell in love with the desert, and never left. I couldn't imagine living anywhere else," Celia replied.

"I've never been to the desert. We always traveled east."

The Jeep created a stream of dust as they left the main highway behind and bounced down a dirt road. When they turned a corner, the ranch opened up suddenly before them, a pop-up vision of southwestern living. The house was a two-story adobe made of red clay, and its edges and corners were rounded, smooth, and uneven. Off to one side were other buildings made of the same material, only smaller.

Celia watched Maggie's face as she looked at the house.

"It's absolutely beautiful."

"Well, it's come a long way since we first bought it."

"Who's *we*?" Maggie asked shyly, awaiting Celia's beautiful spouse to come streaming forth from the house to greet her with art and grace and make Maggie feel stuffy and awkward.

"Liz and I bought it for a song; they practically gave it to us. It was a dilapidated old house then. I bought Liz out a couple of years ago. She's in Vermont now teaching."

"Were you two lovers?" Maggie asked before she could stop herself.

Celia raised an eyebrow, "My, we're inquisitive. Remember, truth-or-dare has its consequences."

"I'm sorry. I didn't mean to pry, and it really is none of my business," Maggie said, grabbing her bag from the back of the Jeep. Her Louis Vuitton luggage was covered in dust from the road, and she inwardly smiled. Harold would have been mortified.

Celia touched her arm. "Don't be. Yes, Liz and I were lovers for fifteen years. In the end things didn't work out."

"I'm sorry."

"It's all right. We had a lot of good times and a lot of growth. Sometimes that means growing apart. Come on, let's get a cold drink and we'll talk."

"Beer?" Maggie inquired.

"Of course, no twelve-steppers here. I'm glad to see life in the Midwest didn't succeed in reforming you."

"A doctor's wife. No, it would spoil the cocktail parties."

Celia smiled and grabbed Maggie's other bag.

17

Once inside, Maggie was led to her room on the second floor. She had to stop herself from wanting to look at and touch everything. Harold had always chided her for being too sensitive to her environment. Celia caught her desire.

"I'll give you the grand tour, and you can fondle as you like."

"Thanks."

Maggie's room was at the end of the hall. It overlooked the courtyard through a large window open to the desert air, sheers fluttering carelessly. There was an antique four-poster bed with a light blue canopy. A large armoire dominated the other corner of the room, and a small writing desk sat next to the window.

"I suppose you found these as awful antiques and redid them?" Maggie inquired.

"Of course. I have a passion for taking misused and forlorn things and making them beautiful again."

"You have made them beautiful," Maggie said, running her hand across the writing desk.

Celia left her to unpack.

She sat on the bed. It felt good to be away. This bed hadn't known Harold and never would; the bathroom wouldn't be filled with his things; the closet and drawers would show no signs of him. Here she would learn to breathe again.

Celia showed her the rest of the house, each room filled with strange artifacts, rugs, antiques. Maggie thought it the most beautiful house she had ever seen, so different from the cherry-wood stuffiness of the Midwest with its elegance and fine china. This was rustic, real, and earthy. Celia was pleased with

Maggie's reactions. Building this house, making it home, had been one of her greatest pleasures.

Celia pulled two Coronas from the fridge and squeezed in some lime juice, saying, "It's a southwestern thing. I hope you like it."

They sat on the veranda, which overlooked the garden. Easing back into the chair, Celia stretched her long tanned legs. Maggie admired their shapely leanness. Nice legs. Celia always had nice legs. All that roaming she used to do.

"Do you still walk all the time?"

"Every morning. Want to come tomorrow? It'll be like old times."

"I'd love to."

Silence ensued. Both felt it acutely.

Maggie looked straight at her. "Are you going to tell me things or do I have to ask embarrassing questions."

"Only if you promise to return the favor. We've got a lot of catching up to do. The question is, do you really want to know?"

"I do. I want to know how you've spent your life. I've always cared about you, Celia, and I've missed you dreadfully."

"I don't really know where to start."

"Start with Liz, since she helped you with this beautiful house."

Celia took a sip. She drew a design with her forefinger in the condensation on the side of the bottle while she meditated on the answer.


Liz, Elizabeth Miller. The mental picture of her

was always the same: standing on the steps outside the Language and Literature Building, sunglasses on, smoking a cigarette, the sun glistening on her dark hair, her head cocked to one side, and her lips smiling. Celia remembered that picture because that was the day she realized she loved Liz.

For an entire year they had been friends, classmates, and drinking buddies, and only occasionally had Celia felt the weight of Liz's gaze, which seemed filled with something akin to sexual energy, until that night. It had been stupid and could have been forgotten, except that it loosed what they both had been denying.

They had been drinking since early afternoon. They had just finished their final exams and were blowing off steam. Celia went to call home. She hung up the receiver and turned around. Liz was standing there, waiting for her.

"Following me now, are you?" Celia had chided. Liz looked at her with such a swelling in her eyes, Celia couldn't help but feel it. Before she knew what happened, Liz kissed her. It wasn't simply a friendly, affectionate kiss; it was a deep, longed for suppression brought suddenly to the surface. Celia closed her eyes and melted into Liz's arms and mouth. When Celia opened her eyes, Liz had disappeared.

For a moment Celia thought she had imagined the whole thing until she saw their empty glasses sitting on the table with no one in sight. Celia walked out of the bar in a daze. She stood in the middle of the sidewalk, trying to decide which way to go.

Habit and fear forced her home. She stayed away

from Liz for two days. A whole two days. Celia commended herself on her willpower. Then she broke. She went out for her morning jog and ran around the university district trying to avoid doing what she knew she would. She arrived at Liz's doorstep. The look they gave each other through the screen door said everything.

"Got a drink for a thirsty soul?" Celia asked.

"Sure," Liz replied, opening the door.

Celia sat on the couch sipping her cranberry juice cocktail and trying to think of what to say. It was strange. It wasn't the first time she had gone running and ended up at Liz's to have a drink. She had always looked forward to it; now she was frightened.

Liz sat next to her. "I'm sorry about the other night. That was way out of line."

Celia looked at her. "Was it?"

"I know that you're involved, and I can't imagine you cheating any more than I can see myself as a mistress."

Liz studied her hands. Celia swirled her drink.

"What happened happened, for a reason I don't think either of us can ignore anymore."

"So where do we go from here?"

"We could have dinner."

"Okay," Liz replied.

That night they made dinner together, settling into a couple without realizing it. Liz had gone shopping and bought the provisions for an epicurean delight. Somewhere in the middle of the dinner preparation they kissed. They ate dinner with pensive, searching eyes that asked, Do you feel like I feel? Do you want like I do? Halfway through washing the dishes, the foreplay started.

Liz stopped them, saying, "I don't want to be a home wrecker but I can't help how I feel."

Celia kissed her in response. "Please take me to bed."

And Liz did. Celia remembered how gently Liz removed her clothes, kissing every part of her, bending her over the bed and making love to every orifice until every part of her had been loved. And Celia loved Liz in return, with Liz on top of her, crying out in ecstasy until they lay in each other's arms. Liz brushed Celia's hair from her face.

"I want you to know that I love you."

Celia started to cry. She couldn't help it. "I love you, too. I can't help loving you; I want to love you."

"I know things are going to be complicated for a while, but I want you to know that I'll wait. I'm willing to wait."

They lay in each other's arms until Liz looked at the clock. "You'd better go. This isn't how she should find out."

Celia went home reluctantly. She pretended to be asleep when Bridgette crawled into bed. Celia silently cried herself to sleep, knowing she had committed what they promised each other would never happen.

For weeks afterward Celia made some incredible ceramic pieces built out of her newfound knowledge of the gamut of love. All the emotions that love inspired touched her in rapid succession. She astounded her classmates, professors, and sometimes herself with the intense erotic nature of her work.

She spent time with Liz when Bridgette was away, and when Bridgette was home Celia found herself being the perfect mate as if making up for her indiscretion. Celia oscillated between grief and elation until guilt set in. It wasn't fair to any of them to keep the game going. Something was going to break.

And it did. It happened one night at the bar, almost by accident. Bridgette had some time off. Celia hadn't seen Liz in a week. She missed her dreadfully. Bridgette, sensing something was wrong, suggested diversion.

They met friends at the bar. The diversion did help. Celia felt the relief of being out and away from what she felt sure was Bridgette's inquiring gaze. It was the same sort of guilt that drove Lady Macbeth to repeatedly wash her hands. Celia couldn't stop thinking about the hideous lie she was living. No matter how hard she tried, she couldn't act normal, she couldn't be herself because she no longer was herself. She was a mess of sticky-sweet emotions.

In the midst of drowning herself in beer and small talk, Celia saw Liz's dark profile across the room. She felt herself drawn toward her. Despite the risk, Celia couldn't stay away. Their eyes met, and Celia made her way across the crowded bar on the pretext of going to the restroom.

Liz watched her and quickly followed. In the back stall, they made hurried passionate love. Celia hadn't meant for that to happen. She only wanted to see Liz, to hold her, to give her body a taste of what it craved. But neither of them could stop. Celia hurried out in a panic, her face flushed, her appearance disheveled.

She met Bridgette's gaze, and then she fled. Bridgette went after her and found Celia crying.

"What's wrong?" Bridgette asked, alarmed.

"If I tell you, you'll hate me," Celia said between sobs.

"It's her, isn't it?"

"What do you mean?"

"I mean you're in love with someone else. Why can't you tell me? Do you think I don't know? That I don't smell her on you when you come home, that I don't know that when I'm not home you're with her, that friends haven't seen the two of you around town? I'm a lot of things, Celia, but I'm not stupid. Learn to say good-bye, and let us both get on with our lives."

"I still love you."

"But not the way you love her. Let's go before things get ugly."

"Are you through with loving me?" Celia asked through tear-stained eyes.

"I'll always love you, but I never expected for us to love each other forever. I always knew someone else would come along."

"You're not sad?"

"Of course I'm sad. Come on, let's go home."

That night they held each other and made love for the last time, crying and laughing about old times. In the morning Bridgette pushed Celia out the door. "Go talk to her and tell her what's going on."

Celia, helpless, looked at Bridgette. "What *is* going on?"

"I'm leaving you or, if you prefer, you're leaving me."

"Am I?"

"I can't be so magnanimous as to let you have a mistress and a wife. Besides, you know as well as I do that we've been companions more than lovers for a long time. Stop being such a coward, Celia, and get on with it."

Celia went running, feeling strange, as if she were running around with a chunk of her soul missing. The even thudding of her shoes on the dirt path and her breathing were the only reminders that she was still there. She didn't go to Liz that night. She made dinner for Bridgette feeling like a somnambulist, going through well-rehearsed motions in order to feel grounded.

Meanwhile, Bridgette was making plans. She wanted to strike out on her own. The realization then came to Celia that her lover had been slowly processing the crisis and dissociating herself in an effort to survive with minimum damage. Celia had thought if anyone broke, it would be Bridgette. But Celia suffered worse. Bridgette went on with her life in good form, wistful when required, strong and practical throughout. Celia had a more difficult adjustment but was luckily rescued by Liz, who quickly discovered the obligatory side of love.

And that was how Celia began the story of how she got together with Liz. She kept eyeing Maggie throughout her narrative, reading from her expressions what her friend might be thinking.

"We had a rather difficult time after Bridgette knew what was going on. I was a basket case. Liz ended up with a mess on her hands. I remember going to her house after spending the afternoon at the bar. I was trying to sort out what had happened.

I threw up on her front lawn and passed out. She had to carry me into the house, clean me up, and put me to bed. In the morning I told her what had happened, that Bridgette was moving out. I half expected her to run, thinking that that should be my punishment for cheating, but she didn't. Instead, she threw herself wholeheartedly into capturing what she referred to as the love of her life. God, I felt like such a shit, like I didn't deserve anyone's love. It was a mess. Then, of course, the community was small enough to know exactly what had gone on. Mutual friends would see both of us about, and I was the cheating bitch, responsible for breaking up the icon couple of the group. And it didn't help that Liz had money. I looked like I was hooking up with a sugar bitch, dumping the brilliant, hard-working love of many years for something better. I was seen as the self-serving asshole."

"Were you?"

Celia took a drink and chuckled. "No. I'm more like a victim of passion. A lot of our friends thought it was lust, but when I ended up in therapy Liz didn't let go. She saw me through it. I think we all realized that lifelong love is not easily obtainable. Bridgette was a saint through the whole thing. She got to know Liz and helped out dealing with my neurotic stage."

"Why neurotic?" Maggie asked.

"I couldn't understand how Bridgette could walk away so easily, always knowing that we wouldn't make it, when I had always expected that we would be together forever. I kept questioning love, asking how people who swore love could give it up and move on with their lives. Why was I devastated by what

26

happened, while Bridgette seemed okay? As I got older I realized that it wasn't that she didn't care, it was that she was a survivor. And survivors carry on. They don't fall apart and torment themselves by asking unanswerable existential questions. I came to understand that love is possible, but it's not necessarily eternal. Bridgette was right all along. Sometimes things aren't quite right, or stop being right, and letting go is the only answer. That's how I got through the split with Liz. We were right. For a long time, we were right. But then something happened — I'm still not quite sure what, but we had to let go."

"That's sad."

"Not really. Once Liz and I got past my insanity, tears, and bouts of blues, we got on really well. We had a good relationship for a long time."

"How did you two finally end it?" Maggie asked, thinking that for all the times she had felt she should leave Harold, knowing that staying was a horrible mistake, she couldn't break through the inertia that immobilized her. She stayed because she lacked the courage that leaving required.

Celia looked at her. "Need another beer?" she said, getting up.

"Please," Maggie replied.

Celia went inside.

Maggie wondered if she had transgressed a hurtful line.

Celia pulled two more Coronas from the fridge and chopped two chunks of lime. Leaving, people leaving. It almost made one not want to fall in love. God, it had hurt knowing that she was losing Liz, but she hadn't known how to make her stay or how

27

to justify a few more years together when they both knew that what they once had, was no longer. Neither was strong enough to make the comfortably neutral into the passion that they needed to survive.

So they had done the squeamish thing and drifted apart before finally letting go. Celia knew that in the past five years after parting, neither had found that elusive lover. They had each taken lovers from time to time, but none of them mattered enough to build a life with. They both yearned for it, and seeing each other fail bothered them, as if they had made a dreadful mistake by not keeping watch over what they had.

Celia didn't want to spend the rest of her life with casual lovers, but she had begun to doubt that she would find the right lover, the one who could keep it all going until they both stopped breathing. She hated to admit it, but her cynicism was becoming a protective shroud that enveloped her heart.

When Celia returned to the veranda, Maggie looked distinctly uncomfortable. Maggie ran her finger around the rim of her bottle and stared off into space, signaling discomfort. Funny how after all these years she retained the same mannerisms.

"What's wrong?"

"Why should something be wrong?"

"Because you have that look."

Maggie shrugged her shoulders. "I'm sorry. I shouldn't have pried."

"Are you prying?"

"Yes."

"Why?"

"Because I asked you to explain the last twenty years in order to fulfill my insensitive curiosity. It wasn't thoughtful to ask about things that might cause you pain."

"It's perfectly understandable. After all, we used to share things all the time. I don't mind, really. But you'll have to do the same. Not right now maybe, but sometime. Deal?"

"Deal."

"I've missed you."

Maggie smiled at her. "I've missed you, too."

Celia told Maggie how the end had come about when Liz got a teaching offer in Vermont. Those were strange days. They knew things weren't good. They had moments of bickering, and they hated that. Neither one of them could admit that it was time to let go, so Liz pretended that she wanted Celia to go with her. Celia declined, to both their relief. They cried, tried to make amends, and made passionate love, but in the end Liz left for Vermont and Celia stayed with the ranch and the studio.

"We tried the long distance thing. For a while it worked okay. It gave our relationship some of the space it was missing. Space in a lesbian relationship is not always obtainable."

"Why do you suppose?" Maggie asked.

"I think it's that woman-mother-sister-nurturer-empathizer thing that makes women so incredible and yet so consumptive of each other. Trying to be someone's everything takes a lot out of a person," Celia replied, thinking about Libby. She didn't give much of herself to Libby because Celia couldn't bear those kinds of feelings any more, and she knew Libby wasn't the right one.

"Do you still miss her, think about her?" Maggie asked.

"Daily. But I have learned some things about myself that I wouldn't have if I'd stayed with Liz. I think about how I went from Bridgette's arms into Liz's without so much as a breather. It is not what I had planned, but sometimes it's nice not to have to worry about how someone else is doing."

Maggie sipped her beer and scanned the horizon. Her own partnership crept into her thoughts.

Her wedding day had had an eerie, surreal quality, as though she were simply observing. It was discomforting to watch her life proceed like a play. She wanted to exit the stage, exit the wings, and exit the theater entirely. But the performance went on.

She stood at the altar in masquerade. After Celia had left, Maggie felt that some part of her had been amputated. She married Harold because his body was an anesthetic. He soothed, placated, and seduced her into being his. She was at a loss to find a reason not to marry him.

"Did you ever cheat on Liz?" Maggie asked Celia.

"No, but it doesn't mean I didn't think about it or that I didn't flirt. Did you ever fuck around?"

Maggie smiled "Let's just say that occasionally I've had invitations, but I never took anyone up. It seemed like it was more trouble than it was worth."

"Of course, now you could with a clean conscience."

"No, I couldn't. I'm done with that."

"Maggie, you're only forty-six. It's pretty early to throw in the towel."

"I wouldn't know how to have another lover, or a spouse. I'm too old to be someone's blushing companion."

"Never say never."

"No, I had my love affair."

Years began to fade as each acquainted the other with what had transpired. Maggie told her about Harold's death, in all its suddenness. They both laughed and cried, agreeing that he was a good man, with Celia thinking he was just not the right person simply because he was a man, and Maggie thinking he was the only man she could have married because Celia had touched him and taught him things — and being with him was a way of being with her.

"Why did you marry him?"

"Why, were you jealous?"

"No, I was happy that you were taking care of him."

Maggie dodged Celia's inquisitive eyes. "Because he was kind to me."

"Do you remember the night you kissed me?"

"Yes."

The conversation, which could have turned into a long-needed confession, was abruptly brought to a close as a young woman sauntered onto the veranda, smiled at Maggie, and kissed Celia lightly on the cheek in an act of ownership. Maggie covered her surprise, and Celia her embarrassment.

"Maggie, this is Libby, one of my apprentices. Libby, this is my friend Maggie."

Libby extended her hand. She was lithe, tanned, and able-bodied with a dazzling white smile and vivid green eyes. Her dark hair was pulled back off her jaunty shoulders.

Celia could tell Maggie was uncomfortable. Although Celia felt angry, she instantly buried any trace of it. Libby knew how to work Celia's emotions in her favor, and Celia had reacted by growing more careful, burying emotions she had once been quick to show. Celia did not like the slant her life was taking. She wondered if having Maggie come was a remedy to get her life on track after the crash-course turns it had been taking.

Libby stayed only a few uncomfortable minutes, and once freed of her presence the two old friends resumed their easy tone. They took leave of each other around midnight. Maggie stood at her open window and gazed at the desert shimmering in the light of a waxing crescent moon. The landscape was empty yet pregnant, and its solitude frightened her. She closed the window and fell into an exhausted sleep that hid her dreams and fears.

She awoke to find Celia holding a tray with a carafe and two cups. The aroma of the rich black coffee permeated the room. Sunlight flooded the room, making the wood floor shine. Maggie gasped at the blueness of the sky as it showed itself through the fluttering sheers.

"It's so blue."

Celia looked out the window. "It is. Bluer than most places. Coffee? You didn't give it up because you lived with a doctor?" Celia asked.

"Please. Can't survive without it."

"So the worrywart didn't cure you of all life's little vices?"

"He tried. Everything in moderation, you know. A lot of good it did him. The bastard died at fifty-six."

Celia cocked her head and crinkled her forehead. "Are you angry about his dying?"

"Wouldn't you be? I planned my life around him, sold my dreams for his safe arms, and he died."

Celia poured the coffee. She was so glad to have Maggie there that she had shamefully forgotten how it had come to be.

"I'm sorry. I guess I'm still processing baggage," Maggie replied.

"Perfectly understandable." Celia smiled.

As they sipped coffee, Maggie's memory wandered back to other mornings when they had sat drinking coffee, back to a time when the two of them existed in happy communion, talking over breakfast and planning adventures. If only life could have stayed so easy, so uncomplicated. Growing up meant that life got progressively more complicated and less pleasurable.

She learned that from Harold. Harold had been convinced that being pained and uncomfortable meant one was living. Maggie hated his fortitude and his diligence. She felt frivolous in the wake of his decisiveness. Her most pleasurable experiences had been with Celia. They had often sustained her when the gravity of being serious, grown-up, and well-behaved threatened to crush her.

Celia tousled Maggie's hair and disrupted her wanderings.

"I thought today we'd pack a lunch and go for a hike in the arroyo. It's part of your desert orientation."

"Wonderful," Maggie replied. Celia left her to her

33

coffee. She needed to coordinate some of the workshop activities before she took a much-needed day off.


Celia found Libby already at work trimming pots. She didn't look up when Celia entered the studio.

"Sanchez order?" Celia inquired.

"Yep. I thought we should complete it by the weekend. Of course, that was before you decided to take a little vacation," Libby replied, letting the wheel come to a slow stop, and looking up.

"Everyone needs some diversion now and then. I figured you could finish the order with no trouble."

"I thought I was your diversion," Libby said, a sardonic smile sliding across her face.

"I could be offended, but why bother if that's how you choose to see what's going on? That's your business. Anyway, I'm going to be gone part of the day. Will you place the supply order and mail the ad copy?"

"In my spare time?"

"Libby, I plan on helping you with the Sanchez order, but you can do most of the prep work. This is, after all, a job. If you don't like the workload, move on," Celia replied, feeling color rise to her cheeks.

"Fine. Please, by all means, go have fun romping with your childhood sweetheart."

"She is not my childhood sweetheart. She's a widow. For chrissakes, Libby, I do have straight friends."

"Then why are you trying to create the island of Lesbos in the middle of the desert?"

"What the hell does that mean?"

"The apprenticeship program this summer."

"Not all woman-centered women are lesbians."

"Just most of them."

"It's about art, Libby. Art should not be practiced in isolation. Besides, the apprenticeship program is how you got here, if you've forgotten."

"Whatever you say," Libby said, kicking the flywheel and resuming her work.

Celia clenched her jaw and suppressed the urge to backhand the nearest piece of greenware. She took a deep breath, stretched her neck from side to side, and walked away. Libby watched from the corner of her eye.


Making lunch, Celia kept thinking about what Libby had said. She was right, of course. Celia did use her for a diversion against the loneliness that sometimes threatened to engulf her. It wasn't healthy for either of them. She had tried to break it off, but somehow Libby managed to stave off the inevitable.

Maggie found her viciously chopping cucumbers.

"Are they dead yet?" Maggie chided.

"Yes," Celia laughed, thinking that chopping food, cooking something, was a way she processed anger. A leftover from therapy, but it worked. It was definitely preferable to screaming fuck you at the top of her lungs and hurling the nearest object across the room. The affair with Libby was over, or it would be over shortly, and Libby would just have to get used to the idea.

\* \* \* \* \*

Celia led Maggie out into the desert chatting amiably. On such a fine day, one should not be bothered by the petty affairs of a fucked-up relationship.

"I wish whacking up cucumbers would put such a bounce in my step."

Celia looked at her slightly alarmed. "You do like cucumber sandwiches?"

"Yes, I love them."

"Libby's such a beast, and sometimes dealing with her makes me a tad cranky."

"So are you two . . ." Maggie asked.

"Lovers? Not exactly. She's infatuated, and I got caught up in that and now I'm regretting it. She has her good points; they just happen to be buried beneath a nasty disposition."

"She's certainly attractive."

"She is. I'll give you that. Come on, we're almost to the edge of the arroyo."

They followed a narrow twisting trail of reddish-black rock downward. The looming saguaros were left behind on the painted plains as smaller plants and ground-hugging cacti of various kinds took their place. The plants, the strange-colored rocks with convoluted surfaces, and the intense blue sky resembled a hallucinogenic illusion. Salvador Dali does the desert, thought Maggie.

"It's all so queer, so different," Maggie said when Celia stopped to empty the pebble that had worked its way into her hiking boot.

"That's why I like it. I can never quite put my finger on why I'm in love, or rapture, with a place

36

most people think desolate and too hot. I like basking in the gentle glow of the mighty fireball," Celia said, laughing and raising her arms skyward, "except maybe when it's a hundred and twelve. But a cool beer on the veranda can make you forget the heat. I do hope that you're falling madly in love with the place," Celia said, her eyes barely perceptible beneath her bandanna and large brimmed straw hat.

"Will it be a moral slam on my character if I don't?"

"No, you wouldn't be the first. Liz thought it was nice but that one place was as good as another. We desert rats are a select few," Celia said, twisting her mouth to one side and shaking her head in resignation.

Maggie smiled. She had forgotten the expressive nature of Celia's face. How she used to laugh at her antics, amazed that anyone's face could be so expressive. Celia had the refined ability of a two-year-old to express in the simplest terms what she was feeling or thinking.

"Well, if I could have a hat like yours, with whatever you have strung around the middle of it, that might just be possible."

"Oh, this," Celia said, bending down to give Maggie a closer look.

"They're shriveled-up lizards," Maggie replied, taking a step backward.

"Precisely, I collect them. All my hats have them."

"And how many hats do you have?"

"Seven exquisitely formed, carefully chosen delights."

"Including this one?"

"Yes, this is number four purchased during a foray in Jerome from a man named Earl who owns the Mexican restaurant and sells hats, stringed chilies, and the hottest salsa in the world."

"This truly is your place," Maggie said as she followed Celia deeper into the arroyo.

"How's this?" Celia asked her, coming to a stop. The stream they had been following spread into a little pool that allowed small trees to grow. They sat on a large, flat rock and dipped their feet into the cool, green pool that lay in contrast to the surrounding hot, dry landscape.

"This tiny little oasis, I don't know. I thought we were going to McDonald's. Did you make a wrong turn?"

"You brat. It's nice to see you smile and laugh."

"You mean I'm transcending your image of the grieving widow? It still doesn't seem real. There were nights I stayed awake so I wouldn't have to see him in my dreams. I used to dream about you, too, after you left."

Maggie picked up a stick and began to dig rocks out of the sole of her boot. "The hardest part about your leaving was that it turned me chicken. I became the coward I always was."

"You didn't like or want to be a doctor's wife?" Celia queried, trying to be sensitive.

Celia knew that Maggie had finished school, had even earned a master's degree, but had done nothing with it. Celia knew Maggie had never done any of the different or outstanding things that she was perfectly capable of doing. When Celia's mother finally got used to the idea of having a lesbian for a daughter, she had looked forward to Celia's mostly infrequent calls. Sally filled her in on all the gossip.

"I never meant to hurt you," Celia said, having a sudden revelation that she was somehow responsible for Maggie's apathy, hoping it was egotism on her part for even entertaining such a notion.

"You did," Maggie said, standing up and walking into the stream, looking out into the desert. "I know that my life should have been good, should have been enough, but it wasn't. I don't know why it felt like a shell for something that could have been deeper, richer, fuller."

"But we all live with some form of nagging disappointment."

Maggie turned to her. "And what was yours?"

Celia found herself stuck for an answer. Either she was the queen of compromise or she hadn't expected any of life's grand notions and had been quite happy with her choices. She knew that the things that drove others didn't drive her. Liz felt differently and had gone questing, leaving Celia in the process.

"I only know some things for certain. Love will not fill the void that a human soul feels. Only a life vision strived for, a sensation felt passionately and nurtured, will bring forth the fruit that fills the hunger created by disappointment. Love, Maggie, will never give you everything you need."

"But it can give you some of what you want."

"Yes."

"And what was, or is, your life vision?"

Celia had a ready answer. "To live on my own terms and in my own way, knowing that is enough."

# Chapter Three

Libby was immediately jealous and felt directly usurped when she walked into the ceramic studio to find Maggie rolling out long clay slabs under Celia's admiring gaze.

"Ruby's Café is expanding. They're putting in a patio section, and Sheryl wants us to do the tabletops. We're going to put Maggie to work, since she's willing."

"And since she's staying," Libby replied with obvious annoyance.

It was true. After a week of good dinners,

morning coffees, walks, and afternoon beers, Maggie looked wonderful. She was tanned and her eyes were clear and well rested. She felt good. Any creeping notions of eventual insanity were banished. And Celia couldn't bear to let her go.

The night before she was scheduled to fly out, Celia had come into her room while she was packing. "I wish you weren't going," Celia said, moving Maggie's suitcase to the other side of the bed and making it difficult for her to continue packing.

"I know. I'm going to miss you, but I'll come back," Maggie replied, holding a pile of clothes ready to be packed. Celia took them from her and sat down on the bed holding them on her lap.

"So why don't you stay for a while longer? The weather is still nasty back there. Why not spend the spring here?"

"And wear out my welcome?" Maggie smiled, thinking it an impossibility.

"I mean it, Maggie. I could teach you to work in the ceramic studio. You seemed interested enough. You'd be working, and the workers live here. Why not you?"

"You're serious?"

"Very," Celia replied. "I like having you around. I want you here for as long as you want to stay. We aborted our friendship once. Let's not do it again."

"What about the ticket?" Maggie asked, picking it from where it lay on the bureau.

"Like that should be a deciding factor," Celia chided. "Take a risk, Maggie. We'll frame it as your first adventurous act in the desert. But answer honestly. Do you want to stay? I'd understand if you want to go back."

Maggie took the clothes back from Celia. "No, you wouldn't. You deserted me once, but that doesn't mean I should do the same. What the hell," Maggie said, pitching the neatly folded pile of shirts over her shoulder. She sat down next to Celia and put her arm around her shoulders. "I don't really need or want to go back. In fact, the thought of it gives me claustrophobia. If you'll take me, I'd love to stay."

"Really?"

"Really and truly. Just throw me out when you're sick of me."

Maggie began her ceramics training the next day. Celia held firm to the conviction that working with one's hands to make things helped cure the malaise that accosted everyone from time to time. Working with clay had helped her more times than she could count. She hoped it would do the same for Maggie.

"Can I talk to you?" Libby asked.

"Outside?"

"How astute you are," Libby replied.

Celia met Maggie's gaze. "I'll be right back."

"So what the fuck?" Libby asked, hands on her hips.

It was times like this that made Celia suppress the urge to smack an insolent daughter. One's lover should not be simulacrum of a daughter. That was evident.

"Don't talk to me like that. If you want to know something or talk about it, have the courtesy to ask in a decent, polite manner."

"Yes, mother."

"That's precisely the problem here, Libby. I don't want to be your mother. I don't want to be your lover. And sometimes you make even being friends difficult."

"What's that supposed to mean?" Libby asked, her knit brows turning her face into a scowl.

The sun was bright, and squinting at Libby was giving Celia a headache. Lately, Libby seemed to have that general effect on her. Celia's neck tensed up and a throbbing at the back of her head would make its slow journey to the temporal area before insistent pain began.

"Libby, get to the point. What's wrong?"

"I thought I was your assistant."

"For chrissakes, Libby, Maggie's just helping out, and this isn't a corporate-ladder scene. We all work together. Get used to it or get out." Celia walked back into the studio. She heard the slam of the truck door and the spinning tires. Libby's usual manner whenever they fought was to charge off in that damn truck. I should let the air out of the tires next time we get to bickering, Celia thought.

Celia walked into the studio, saw a particularly convenient piece of greenware, and backhanded it off the table.

She shrugged her shoulders. "Ah, much better," she said, smiling at Maggie. "Now, where were we?"

"Are you all right?"

"No. Actually I need an aspirin or, better yet, a joint."

"You don't smoke dope still?"

"Only occasionally, and right now seems like one of those occasions," Celia replied, pulling a joint out of a drawer. "Come on, let's go out back. It'll be fun.

43

Then we'll cut tiles. The slabs need to get hard anyway."

They sat in the covered arbor attached to the studio. Maggie found herself getting giddy just like she used to when, just as illicitly, they used to sneak off and blow a spliff without Harold knowing. It was their secret, and they used to laugh about how horrified he'd be if he knew.

"I'm sure Harold used to do some things that would horrify us, " Celia said.

"Harold?" Maggie answered. "I think you have him confused with someone else. Harold never did a dishonest thing in his entire life."

They looked at each other and burst into laughter.

"You're right."

"Do you have a local drug dealer?" Maggie asked, wondering what it was like to be middle-aged and buying pot.

"Oh, God no, I grow it in the garden with the rest of the herbs."

"You're just like Mrs. Madrigal in Maupin's *Tales of the City*."

"I feel like that sometimes, but what are you doing reading stuff like that?" Celia said smiling.

"It was on PBS. I may be straight, but —"

"You're not narrow."

Later that night Celia couldn't sleep. She went to the studio and worked on the tiles. Libby saw the light and went out to her. Celia was perched on a high stool meticulously cutting the tiles and listening to music, completely absorbed in her thoughts. She felt Libby's touch on her shoulder, her lips on her bare neck, her soft breath saying, "Don't be mad. I'm sorry about this afternoon."

"Libby, this really has got to stop," Celia said.

"I know. I'm sorry. I just want to spend some time with you," Libby said, tears welling up in her sparkling green eyes.

"Don't do that," Celia said, brushing them away and kissing Libby's forehead. "Libby, I can't love you. I don't know what's wrong, but I can't. Please try to understand." She drew Libby to her and tried to make the tears stop, tried to make the hurt go away.

"I'll take whatever you can give, please don't let me go. I need you."

Celia looked at the tearstained face of her lover. "You only make it harder."

"I love you, dammit. I can't make it go away simply because you don't want it anymore."

Celia held her, kissed her, allowed her lust to be roused. "I'm sorry, I'm so sorry. I wish I could make things different," Celia told her, unable to be what her lover needed.

They kissed and held each other. They went inside to get some beer before sitting by the pool. They swam and lay naked in each other's arms.

"Promise me you'll relax and just let us be."

Libby looked up at Celia, her eyes bright with love. "Anything. You know I'll do anything."

Celia kissed Libby and rolled back into the pool. Libby followed.

Upstairs, Maggie awoke from a dream, another one filled with images of Harold. Hearing voices by the pool, she got up. She stood at the window. Libby and Celia. The dim light from the kitchen illuminated the perimeter of the pool. Maggie heard Celia laugh and saw her gently push Libby away. Libby came back and back again until Celia wrapped her arms around her and did not let go. In the translucent blue water, under the light of the moon, the two women pleased each other. Maggie watched, unable to pry herself from her vantage point.

When the lovemaking was over, the two women lay on a towel near the water's edge holding each other. Celia stroked Libby's dark hair and kissed her eyes and mouth. Soon enough, they were enwrapped again. Maggie wondered at their stamina.

Celia also wondered, at Libby's ability to bewitch. Every time she thought she could get away, could wean Libby away from their strange arrangement, Libby would prostrate herself, make amends, then seduce Celia to the point where she was unable to stop drowning in Libby's lovely body.

"The only thing we do well together is make love," Celia said, lying back on the towel, sweaty and spent.

"And argue and kiss and work and be selfish and guarded. We do those things well too."

"Libby, you deserve more than this. Someone your own age, someone to share everything with, someone to start a life with."

Libby did something quite out of the ordinary. Instead of engaging in dialogue, she put her finger to Celia's lips to quiet her and said, "Just hold me."

This made Celia more apprehensive than an argument. Had they argued, she could have consoled herself that they were ill matched. Celia honestly didn't know why she couldn't fall in love with Libby.

She couldn't seem to get past lusty infatuation. She tended to blame the situation on Libby, but now she was beginning to wonder if she herself was the problem.

Maggie felt enlightened. So that's what they do, she thought. From time to time the mechanics had crossed her mind, but the visuals certainly exceeded any diagram.

Maggie tried to remember the last time she had sex. The sexual part of her relationship with Harold had certainly fizzled from what had never been great. In fact, she had seduced Harold the first time. After that she usually had to remind him that getting laid once in a while was part of the bargain.

She eventually taught him enough tricks to satisfy her, so she guessed it was an okay erotic life. But that display by the pool was enough to convince her that there was much more to it. She was curiously aroused.

She lay back on the bed, moving her hand down her breasts, feeling their firmness, stroking the nipples until they were erect. She ran her hand across and down her still taut stomach, finding her jutting hipbones. She had lost ten pounds since Harold died, and she hadn't been fat to begin with. She touched the mound of hair and ran her fingers down the lips, gently parting them. Lifting her nightshirt, she caressed herself and put her fingers inside. She was wet, and entering was easy. She rolled on her stomach and thrust inside until she felt her body quiver. She fell into a deep sleep.

\* \* \* \* \*

Voices from downstairs and sunlight dancing on her eyelids told her it was day. Maggie put on her robe and went downstairs for coffee. Libby sat at the table wearing one of Celia's denim shirts, chatting amiably. Maggie observed her dark, disheveled hair and felt a slight pang of jealousy. Libby was attractive, the embodiment of rollicking sensuality and, from last night's display, obviously very good at it. Maggie felt frumpy in comparison. Celia, however, did not look quite so glowing. She seemed tired and restless. Relief came in a smile when she saw Maggie.

"Coffee and juice?" Celia asked, starting to get up.

"I'll get it," Maggie said, wandering toward the kitchen.

"No, sit down. Let me," Libby said, jumping up.

Maggie and Celia made eye contact with a mutual look of surprise.

"All right," Maggie replied.

Libby was perfectly charming all morning. When she went off to shower before starting work, Maggie and Celia sat dazed by the turnabout behavior.

"What did you do to her? I don't think I've ever seen that side of Libby."

"You don't want to know. Wait, it won't last."

Maggie thought suddenly, I know and wish I didn't. She was puzzled to hear Celia say, "I'm really rather embarrassed about all this."

"About what?"

"Being involved with someone so much younger. I feel like one of those dirty old men attracted to fresh young things. Do I look absurd? I want an honest answer."

"No, you don't look like a dirty old man. How much younger is she?"

"Fifteen years. I could be her mother."

"Not unless it was a teenage pregnancy. If it doesn't bother her, why should it bother you? I wouldn't worry about it."

"What would you have me worry about?" Celia chided.

"How you're going to turn your cowardly widowed friend into a swinging single."

Celia laughed. "We'll see what we can do. Last I heard, you'd given up on all that."

"Things change."

"True, Libby was actually civil to you this morning."

Libby was civil for a lot longer than Celia thought she was capable. She began to resemble the woman Celia had once known. Celia found herself having a difficult time not reciprocating, and for a time she let herself go with it. It wasn't love, but it was companionship.

The three women got on. They went for walks, and a picnic. They went into town and found Maggie a desert hat. They fell into an easy rapport with one another. Being three helped their relationship.

But all blissful triangles come to an end. The way Celia and Maggie looked at each other and the way they were playfully chummy caught Libby's attention, and she began to call Celia on it.

\* \* \* \* \*

"She's not even a dyke. I don't see where you're getting these ideas. We're old friends for chrissakes."

"She wouldn't be the first woman to change her mind after being married. No one is safely heterosexual. No one is safely off-limits. And that includes Maggie."

"I thought you liked her," Celia lamely replied, wondering herself if she could be entirely trusted.

"Even if I like her, she can still steal my girlfriend."

"No, Libby, you're being absurd. Relax. I'm not fucking anyone but you. It's nice and I like it. Don't wreck it. Okay? You and only you. Platonic relationships are perfectly ordinary and possible."

"All right, for now," Libby replied, pointing at her from across the studio floor.

Celia looked at her lover quizzically. "What's that? Don't point at me. I'm too old to be reprimanded, especially by you. Since when are you in charge? When did I lose control of this relationship?" Celia smiled as she went across the room to nestle between Libby's long legs. She kissed her neck and her breasts and unzipped her shorts. It wasn't the first time Celia buried lust for one woman in the arms of another.

"What about Maggie?" Libby asked, suddenly shy about her lover's advances.

"She's on the phone with Amanda, and I'm sure it's not pretty," Celia said, undaunted in her pursuit. Amanda, from what Celia had deduced from various frantic phone calls, was a wordy one. Whom she got it from she would never know. Neither Harold nor

Maggie were blabbermouths. Maybe Amanda did the talking for all three of them. Amanda had been checking in on her mother weekly ever since Maggie failed to return as scheduled. Amanda, it seemed, didn't take highly to surprises.

"What's the deal? She's a big girl. Has her own apartment, boyfriend, and such. Right?"

"Yes. I don't understand it myself. If she doesn't want to watch the house anymore, Maggie could hire someone, sublet the damn thing."

At that moment, Maggie walked into the studio. Libby, catching the spark in Celia's eyes when she saw Maggie, smiled wryly before zipping up and leaving.

"I wish she'd get off my back," Maggie said. "This reversal of roles is really getting on my nerves. Is this what children do? Grow up to boss their aging parents?"

"Libby reprimanded me today. Pointed her finger at me."

"Young people today. Another beer, madame?"

"I don't know. I think I'm starting to feel rather good."

"That's the point," Maggie said, handing her a cold wet beer.

Celia ran it across her forehead. "I guess I could be persuaded into having another."

"What did you do that was so terribly wrong?" Maggie asked, sitting nonchalantly in a wicker chair. The water from the mister felt good on her bare shoulders.

"Libby thinks we're getting a little too chummy. She thinks I'd like to hop into your shorts."

Maggie choked, showering them both with her beer. When she recovered her composure, she looked up and smiled. "Would you?"

"Maggie, I would never jeopardize our friendship in that way. You're too much of a lady, and I wouldn't know how to act."

"And you're afraid I wouldn't know what to do."

"It's not hard. Believe me."

Maggie smiled, thinking she'd be in trouble if Celia could read minds.

Later that night, Maggie lay outstretched on her bed, arms behind her head, thinking about what Celia had said. One overwhelming thought kept coming to mind. Was their relationship as platonic as they both liked to think? Was she even a woman-identified woman?

She hadn't many female friends, and most often they had been wives of Harold's colleagues. She felt socially awkward when other women rattled on about their families because she was less interested in hers and less fulfilled. It must have shown. The women shied away from her and sought more suitable acquaintances.

Maggie wanted to stay with Celia long enough to meet the apprentices. She needed to know if suburbia and suburban wives or her own inadequacies created her alienation. She got along with Libby well enough despite Libby's suspicions. At least they could talk about ideas and opinions on the state of existence, art, literature, all sorts of things — and those things mattered to Maggie.

She knew one thing for certain. She liked being there, and if Celia spent each summer surrounded by women, Maggie could certainly be one of those women. No amount of persuasion on Amanda's part could send her back now. Something within Maggie had been unleashed, and that something wasn't willing to be tethered again. Amanda would have to get used to the idea.

"Today I want to teach you to throw," Celia said.

"Oh, no. I'm not coordinated enough. Flat things are my forte," Maggie replied, remembering her success with the tile tabletops. They were beautiful, and she was proud of them.

But Celia ignored her protests. She helped Maggie make several balls of clay the size of oranges. "We start with cylinders."

Celia watched as Maggie tried to manage the miscentered wad of clay.

"See, I told you," Maggie said as her fourth attempt failed.

"Let me help you," Celia said. She sat behind Maggie at the wheel. Together they molded the clay, bringing it up, pressing it down, centering it on the spinning wheel.

"You know what this reminds me of?"

"Yes, it reminds everyone of that, but the movie scene had a real potter do the throwing."

"It was a sensuous scene. I never thought I'd be doing anything close to this."

"Unfortunately, there won't be a seduction following," Celia said.

"Shucks," Maggie said, feeling Celia's strong arms as they cradled her own, her breasts pressing against Maggie's back, her breath warm on her neck.

Celia smiled as Maggie tried to manipulate the unwieldy brown mass in front of her. Celia's trained hands slowly steadied Maggie's tentative ones.

"I've got the wrong parts, remember?" Celia replied.

"Are you so sure about that?"

"If I didn't know you better, I'd think you were flirting with me," Celia replied.

"Shhh, Libby won't take highly to that. Too chummy."

"Chummy is all we've got."

"Whose fault is that?" Maggie joked.

"At the moment, I'd say it was Libby's."

"If I didn't know better I'd think *you* were flirting with *me,*" Maggie replied.

"I would never."

"And why not?"

"I've too much respect for your mind."

"I would never stoop to something so trivial as flirtation. Thanks for making me feel undesirable."

"Oh, you're far from undesirable."

"Then what am I?"

Celia's reply was cut off as Libby slammed the door and scowled at them. Libby demanded that Celia help her unload the truck now. Celia would like to have answered Maggie by saying something to the effect that she was a sensuous woman with a nice body, beautiful eyes, warm kissable mouth, and breasts that Celia wished she could scoop up and suckle.

It was a good thing Libby came in when she did.

* * * * *

Celia sat at her desk with her palms resting in her eye sockets. Libby had nailed her ass to the wall about the chummy private lesson. How long could Celia sustain ignorance? She felt something like desire for her best friend, who, for purposes of reference, was straight. Were they really just kidding around, or was it some kind of verbal foreplay?

Was it a good idea to be toying around with a straight woman's sense of sexuality? A forty-six-year-old baby dyke. The best way to get your heart broken. The confusing part was that Maggie was not necessarily an unwilling participant. They had steered clear of each other for a few days, and when they talked about it again Maggie apologized for causing friction.

"I don't mean to come between you two."

"Maggie, it's not like that."

"I can't say that if I was Libby I wouldn't feel the same way. You two have been out here by yourselves, and then I come along and mess with things. But she must know it's not like that. I'm not trying to steal her girlfriend."

"You mean you're just a tease?" Celia said, trying to divert the conversation with humor.

"Celia," Maggie said, looking at her seriously.

Celia suppressed the urge to say, Do you know how sexy you are when you do that? Almost as instantly as that question sprang to mind, she knew she'd better put a lid on it or there would be big trouble on the ranch, namely, that Maggie would pack up, scared as shit that her long-lost dyke pal tried to seduce her. "I'm sorry. But Christ, this is really getting old. You know what I'd like. I'd like to be in love with a woman, an adult, someone who didn't fly into jealous rages over every little thing and think everything I do is a provocation."

"I know. I'm sorry. I don't want to cause trouble."

Celia looked at her, squelching her desire to throw herself prostrate at Maggie's feet and say, Why can't I admit to loving you? I know I want you, but you're not like that. It's my own craziness. Say something to make it go away. Tell me I'm being foolish. That you're flattered and all that, but it can't be. "No, don't be sorry. We're not doing anything wrong. She's being possessive, and I don't like it. If she makes me choose, she'll be the one to go. I'm sorry you have to experience one of my mistakes."

"Is it a mistake?"

"Yes, and the sooner it's over, the better. I just wish I wasn't such a coward."

"A coward? I always see you as heroic."

"If I was heroic I would simply tell her it was nice but it's over."

"It is never that easy. You don't like to hurt people, so being that abrupt is not in your nature," Maggie said, walking over and putting her arms around Celia's shoulders."

"Let's go for a swim. I'm hot and tired. There's no pleasing Libby, so we might as well piss off the rest of the afternoon. I am the boss."

"Okay, boss lady. Let's go."

* * * * *

The intimate sharing and withdrawal under careful scrutiny of a third party confused them both.

Maggie tried to steer herself away from Celia and Libby to give them time alone. Libby took it as an act of faith that Celia and Maggie were simply friends, that Maggie was straight.

Maggie knew she had begun to tell herself lies again. The sheen she had so recently felt enveloping her life was becoming cloudy, except when she was around Celia. Maggie knew that her eyes told truths her mouth denied. She was afraid that if Celia looked into them, she would read the secreted truth.

Celia understood what Maggie was trying to do, so for a while she paid attention to Libby, taking her for walks, potting with her, getting her to help in the large garden. But Libby enjoyed none of those things. She acquiesced when she was feeling generous, but they both knew it was an effort. The only time they came together was when they made love. It was then they talked to each other and made allowances. Celia apologized with her body and breathlessness for not loving Libby, and Libby understood that her body was all Celia could offer. Though it made her ache, Libby began to know that Celia didn't withhold her love because she was mean and manipulative but because she didn't have anything to give anymore.

Celia now admitted to herself that she had kept Libby on because she was lonely and missed having someone around. Waking up to an empty house or going home to it was too sad.

Her previous self-imposed isolation had bothered her. Her desert home needed the barefoot slapping of many feet, the tinkling of many voices. That was why she had started the summer apprenticeships, so she would have women around her.

The little art community worked. She had women around, and they weren't lovers. And that was pleasant. She could be the charming queen of the house, flirt in harmless attraction, and have women come and go with an occasional tumble and few complications. Libby was the exception, but that was due to her attractive tenacity.

Celia admired Libby's stubborn courage. But she wanted to be with Maggie. She enjoyed her company most, and she could do things with Maggie that she couldn't do with Libby. But triangles don't last; they tumble like houses of cards. One person always left for one reason or another.

One day Maggie would leave, and Celia dreaded it. She would have the summer, but the house always emptied itself in the fall. Maggie would go home, and Libby, or someone else like her, might stay. Celia would feel the loneliness and creeping sense of loss again.

Celia closed the book and held it to her chest, wishing she could stop feeling the dread. She couldn't tell Maggie that she wanted her to stay, to live here, to be the one that made her feel complete and not lost. Lovers, not friends, stay together. Friends get dragged off by lovers. Celia couldn't expect that Maggie would live a celibate life on the outskirts of

Celia's love affairs. But it didn't seem possible that there could be anything else.

Her gloomy thoughts were broken by a soft tap on the door frame.

"Can't sleep?" Celia asked. Maggie stood in a nightshirt, her hair disheveled about her shoulders.

"How was your evening?" Maggie asked.

"It was okay." Celia and Libby had gone into town, eaten dinner, and seen a movie. "I missed you," Celia added, patting the bed. "Come sit down."

"What are you reading?"

Celia showed her the cover.

"Is it good?"

"Yeah," Celia replied, putting the book down. "Maggie, what's wrong?"

Maggie looked at her and started to cry. Celia put her arms around Maggie and switched out the light. Celia didn't ask questions. They both knew what it was about. They lay back, not saying anything for several long minutes.

Then, "Celia?"

"Yes."

"I missed you tonight. I can't go on existing on the periphery. I'm tired of being alone."

"I know."

"I'd better go."

"No, don't go. Stay. We'll be two old, lonely women together."

"But you have Libby."

"It's possible to have someone and be lonely, sometimes even lonelier."

"But —"

"Shhh, let's rest."

When Celia heard Maggie's deep and regular breaths, she too fell asleep, glad that Maggie was close by.

They were still sleeping when Libby found them. Celia's arm hung loosely across Maggie's side, her face nestled close. Libby strode from the room in silent fury.

The sound from downstairs of slamming coffee cups woke Celia. She heard the coffee decanter being thrust into its cradle and knew Libby had seen them. It was late. Celia rolled on her back and listened to Maggie's even breathing, watching the serenity that sleep had brought to her face.

Oh, Libby, why must you move with such anger and force through your own life and mine? I don't want your anger, your rage at the world for not being like you want it. You don't know *what* you want, only *that* you want. I can't give you the answer. My lust and your desire will not deliver you from your own passions, Celia thought as she crept out of bed.

She wished she would be there when Maggie awoke, that she could stroke her hair, kiss her sleepy eyes, and smile deeply into her soul. Reluctantly, she went downstairs to face what she knew would be a very unhappy woman. It wouldn't have looked good to Libby, but it had been innocent. Celia wouldn't lie and say she hadn't enjoyed it. She had wanted Maggie there.

"Good morning," Celia said, sensing the imminent barrage.

Libby scowled at her. "What the fuck is going on? Are you two sleeping together and just haven't gotten around to telling me?"

Celia poured herself a cup of coffee, vying for time. Maybe she should let Libby think something was going on so it would be over. But she knew that wouldn't work. Libby would confront Maggie, and Maggie wouldn't lie. What would that do to Maggie? Would it frighten her to be implicated in such a sordid affair? Just because she spent the night in your bed doesn't mean she would fuck you.

Celia looked glumly back at Libby. "It wasn't like that, won't be like that. So drop it."

"Maybe you're wishing it was like that."

"Libby, you don't own my life. I'm not obligated to explain anything to you. Maggie is my friend, and sometimes friends need each other. Think what you like."

"I think you'd like to fuck your best friend, only you don't have enough courage to admit it. You're both hypocritical cowards, saying one thing when you really feel quite different." Libby glared at Celia. "It doesn't matter what happens to us. I'm just the excuse you use not to confront your feelings for her. It doesn't matter that I love you, that I want you,

61

that it drives me crazy when you keep me at arm's length, that you let her in your bed but not me. I don't mean shit to you!" Libby slammed the door behind her.

"I hate door slammers," Celia said to an empty room.

"Me too. Amanda slams doors," Maggie said.

Celia looked up. Maggie stood on the stairs.

"Maybe we should introduce those two."

"Pity they're of opposite persuasions."

"Yeah, I guess that's the underlying current around here."

"Is it?"

"You tell me."

"I don't know how."

"One of us should probably learn then. Coffee?"

"Please."

# Chapter Four

The tavern was relatively quiet when Maggie, Celia, and Celia's friend Karen took stools at the bar. It was early afternoon, and most of the locals were still working. Maggie admired the ceiling, which was made of ornate copper tiles.

Celia and Maggie had left Libby sulking at home and driven to Jerome with a shipment of dinnerware. Jerome had been a mining town, then a ghost town, and now it was a mecca for gay and lesbian artists and entrepreneurs. Maggie was stunned by the majestic beauty of Jerome. The gentrified town sat high on a red cliff and possessed a view that seemed to go on forever. They took the shipment to the gallery that Karen owned and operated.

Karen Thomas was a tall woman, an impressive personality in well-tailored clothes. She wore her dark hair in a tight bun. Her long neck was accented by a sculpted brooch that closed her white silk shirt. She was the richest woman in Jerome, and she commanded respect wherever she went, Karen Thomas was not a woman to cross. She thought the world of Celia and worked hard to sell her work.

"Where's the snot-nosed brat?" Karen asked.

"Libby is sulking at home."

"What did you do this time?"

Celia looked at Maggie, who sat on the other side of Karen. Maggie raised her eyebrows and looked around.

"I'm not paying her enough attention, and she's jealous that I prefer Maggie's company."

"Which is perfectly understandable, since Libby's such a pain in the ass. No offense, Maggie. Libby makes me wonder what happened to give her such an attitude. The grinch could not possibly have stolen her Christmas every year."

"I don't know. She won't talk about anything in the past. What's done is done as far as she's concerned."

"Sounds like someone in need of therapy — or someone who gave up on too much therapy. Anyway, we should have ourselves a good ole time tonight. Before we call it an evening and head back to the ranch, we should buzz into Phoenix and hit a few bars. I haven't been out in ages," Karen said, pouting.

Celia didn't exactly point in Maggie's direction, but Karen got the gist.

"Oh, darling, you're not straight are you?"

"Why, won't they let you in the bar?"

"Good comeback. I can see we're going to get along just fine. Witty and daring are my favorite flavors. So you don't mind going out to play with Aunt Karen?"

"You don't have to go," Celia said.

"No, I want to. I haven't been out to play for a long time."

"You do understand what kind of a bar we're talking about?" Celia inquired.

"Yes, maybe we should lay a wager to see who gets a date first."

"Maggie!" Celia said.

"I was just kidding."

"It's never too late, darling, to switch sides. I saw you turning heads today."

"Karen, stop it."

"You're awfully protective, Celia. Is there something I should know about you two?"

"Drink your beer."

"Yes, mommy."

Karen insisted they leave the truck and take her Jaguar sedan to town. "I do not ride in trucks, and this way I will spend a few days at the ranch and then drive one of you back, preferably Maggie. We need to talk."

There was no arguing with Karen as they drove an average speed of ninety toward Phoenix. Maggie was more than slightly apprehensive about going to a gay bar And once in the parking lot of The Biz, she admitted her fright.

"All first experiences create fright, even birth, but we all survived that. Give it an hour, then we'll talk."

Celia took her hand, "A bar's a bar, only this one is full of women."


Maggie felt acutely self-conscious as she put her Corona to her lips. Karen watched her. Celia was trading gossip with the bartender.

"So you were married?"

Maggie still wore her wedding ring. She hadn't given it much thought. She twisted it on her finger.

"I guess I am a marked woman."

"Where is he now?"

"He died last year."

"Oh, death. Definitely a twenty-questions faux pas. I'm sorry."

"I don't know why I still wear it. Habit, I guess."

"So are you picking up any new habits hanging around with a bunch of dykes?"

"A change of heart, you mean?"

"Yes."

"I wouldn't be the first, would I?"

"No. Nor will you be the last."

"Were you always a lesbian?"

Karen signaled to the bartender for two more Coronas.

"No, I was married once, to a stockbroker in

California. I ran a gallery there and fell in love with a talented young female artist. Strangest thing I ever did, but it was the right thing. I realized a lot about myself, moved to Jerome, and have lived quite happily ever since."

"Are you living together now?"

"Oh, no, my darling. I'm easily bored, and home-on-the range is not my scene. Not yet, at least. Let's just say I have a few girlfriends, and we understand one another for the most part. I'm not into complications."

"Oh," Maggie replied, not knowing what else to say.

"I'm not all that bad. I'm just hell to live with. Come dance with me."

"Do I have to?"

"Yes."

Maggie felt herself letting go as she became part of the mass of sweating, throbbing humanity moving to the primordial beat. Sweaty and smiling, Karen and Maggie returned to the bar.

Celia looked on curiously. "Do you like it?"

"Yeah," Maggie said, slipping to Celia's slang. Harold had hated *yeah* and insisted on *yes.* But Maggie liked the way Celia said it, a lingering, well-thought-out response. Yeah. Emphatic and full of life.

She looked around, scanning the crowd. It was a diverse group. Women laughing, talking, kissing, making up, and inevitably breaking up. Couples, old and new, the tender and the hard-hearted, the wounded and the slingers of arrows. It wasn't so different, and it wasn't so scary. It wasn't the bizarre underground life she'd been led to believe.

On the way home Celia and Karen told her dyke

stories, the funny and the sad stories of themselves and their friends. Slightly drunk, Maggie laughed hysterically.

Maggie lay in bed thinking back over the stories and their lighthearted sadness. The idea of accepting one's course in life without regret struck Maggie with sudden force.

I want to be like that. Maggie smiled into the darkness of her room, and sat up hungry. It felt good to be hungry after seeing and experiencing new things.

She didn't bother to switch on the light in the kitchen. She preferred the serenity of the darkness; the dark gave mystery to the objects in the room; the light stole dark's autonomy in its blanket visibility. Maggie thought she was alone until she saw the burning orange end of Karen's cigarette from across the room.

"I thought I heard someone up," Karen said. "Couldn't sleep?"

"I was suddenly hungry."

"What are you making?" Karen asked as Maggie pulled stuff from the fridge.

"A sandwich. Want one?"

"Please. Do you have any provolone?" Karen said as she stepped behind Maggie to peer in the fridge.

Their sandwiches made, they sat on the couch and ate.

"You're staying the summer?"

"Yes, I'm taking a hiatus from my real life."

"And what is your real life?"

"I don't know anymore."

"Maggie, I want you to stay with me for a few days. You're living in an isolated moment here, it would be a good idea to step out and get some renewed perspective. I'll take care of everything, so there is nothing to be frightened of. Okay?"

"Okay."


Celia stood holding the coffee pot in midair looking utterly dismayed.

"You're doing what?"

"I'm going to spend a few days in Jerome with Karen. I just think it would be a good idea."

Celia knew it was Karen's idea, and she couldn't quite figure out the reasoning behind it. But Karen was like that, a strange instigator.

Celia smiled and said, "Well, I'll miss you dreadfully. You will be coming back?"

Maggie walked over and slung her arm casually over Celia's shoulders. "Of course. I wouldn't want to lose the best quarters in the house to another wandering guest."

"Maggie, I don't want you to be a guest. I want you to live here — even if it's just for a while — for as long as you like. Think about it, okay?" Celia said, her eyes full of the intensity of the request.

"Only if I can have some java," Maggie said, smiling and holding out her empty coffee mug.

"I mean it."

"I know you do."

Celia watched Maggie and Karen pull out onto the dirt road, and she felt suddenly lonely. Maybe being left again was what she needed to startle her into some form of action.

Climbing the winding road to Jerome, Maggie looked at the digital clock on the dashboard and thought about Celia, wondering what she was doing.

Karen looked over at her between maneuvering curves. "Miss her already?"

"Who?" Maggie replied absently.

"You know."

"Queer, isn't it?"

"Appropriate, I think."

Karen's rambling three-story house was nestled among foliage on a secluded hillside at the edge of town. Karen gave Maggie a room on the third floor beneath dormer windows that looked out at desert valleys and mountaintops.

Maggie put her sandals on, then lay back on the bed, her arms folded behind her head, to wait for Karen to call her. They were going to dinner at a friend's.

Julia and Sidney's house was on the other end of town. It was half living quarters and half art gallery. One side was glass from floor to roof and overlooked the entire valley, a postcard vision of nature.

After dinner they had coffee on the deck. Maggie found herself thinking about Celia and how much she had come to like doing the woman thing, making dinner, having coffee, talking. No pressure, just the simplicity of likeness. She admired and envied Julia and Sidney with their well-honed lifestyle. It all seemed so pleasant and organized.

Afterward on the street Karen asked, "What did you think?"

"About what?"

"Julia and Sidney, the whole couple thing."

"Is that what dinner was all about? Educating me into the ways of lesbian life? If it was, it was hardly necessary. You're not selling me on anything I haven't already realized."

"And what have you realized?"

"That my life is taking on a sense of direction and that if I hang out with one person long enough I'll probably change my hairstyle to match my significant other."

Karen laughed. "You do have to admit they are awfully cute, little matching versions of each other with slight alterations. But that is what is so humorous. It's to be expected, though. Live with someone long enough, and you get to look like her."

"Is that why you don't do the couple thing? No sapphic likenesses for you?"

"What an astute woman you are. Broken molds have difficulty finding perfect matches. I'm still open, honey."

They walked in the moonlight through the quiet streets.

Passing the local bar, Karen insisted they have a nightcap. They sat talking to the flamboyant bartender who filled their ears with local gossip until two in the morning. Maggie thought it funny that everyone Karen introduced her to assumed that she was a lesbian. And she didn't really care to straighten the matter out.


On the third day of Maggie's absence, Celia forced herself to talk to Amanda. Although she had dodged her for the better part of a week, this time she answered the call. She picked up the phone seconds before Amanda began the tedious list of her activities. She wanted her mother to know just where to find her and at what hour, indicating in each message that she expected a prompt response.

"Celia, is my mom there?"

"No, Amanda. She went to Jerome to stay with a friend for a few days."

"What friend? She didn't tell me she had any other friends there except you."

"This is a new friend, Amanda."

"She went to stay with someone she just met?" Amanda said, incredulous that her mother would do such a thing.

"In a manner of speaking, yes. But Karen is an old friend of mine."

"Let me get this straight. This woman is a friend of yours, but you didn't go with them. My mom is with someone she hardly knows in a strange town. Is this place still in Arizona?"

"Yes, it's just up the road."

"When is she coming back?"

"Soon."

"When is that?"

"Amanda, contrary to your notions, your mother is a grown woman, quite capable of taking care of herself. If she wants to go off somewhere and see some new things, it shouldn't really concern you."

"Well, she's not that stable, you know."

"What does that mean?"

"I mean that after Dad died she got kind of freaky. In fact, one day I found her outside burning Dad's shoes."

Celia smiled. Oh, Maggie, you naughty little creature. "I'm sure she had a good reason."

"For torching a pair of shoes?"

"Amanda, you need to get on with your own life and leave your mother's alone. I'll have her call you when she gets home."

"Isn't there a number where I can reach her?"

"No, I'm afraid the nudist colony doesn't allow phone calls."

"What!"

"Good-bye, Amanda," Celia said as she replaced the receiver.

Libby found Celia chuckling to herself.

"What could possibly be so amusing?" Libby asked.

"I have a better question. What happened to your generation to make you all so uptight and humorless?"

"Don't fuck with me," Libby snarled as she left the room.

Celia looked out the window, thinking, No, my darling, I shan't any longer.

Life at the ranch wasn't the same without Maggie. Celia and Libby were at each other's throats without Maggie's pacifying presence to temper their behavior. They were forced to acknowledge how bad things had become. Every moment together was a strain, so they avoided each other.

The sky turned crimson and orange as Celia sat by the pool. If Maggie was here we would be sitting together, yakking up a storm, watching the sunset.

Instead, she saw Libby, dirty from the clay, leaning against the studio, smoking a cigarette. Why do relationships get like this? One standing here, one there, and nothing to say between them? Celia went inside to get another beer. Getting slowly tanked by the pool seemed like a good idea.

In the middle of her ruminations, she became possessed with the idea of talking to Maggie. She would admit to missing her because she knew now that that was Karen's purpose in keeping Maggie. Karen obviously thought that there was more to their friendship than either Celia or Maggie was willing to admit.

"Hello." Karen's voice jingled over the line.

"Hi, how's it going up there?" Celia asked, trying to be casual. If she blamed the call on Amanda she might be able to slink past Karen's over-inquisitive mind.

"Missing someone?"

"How is she doing?"

"She's the new belle in town. I've been asked several times if she's up for grabs."

"Well, she's not."

"Why? Are you laying claim?"

"Karen, please, just let me talk to her," Celia said, trying to keep exasperation and frustration from creeping into her voice.

Maggie picked up the phone, feeling a little flushed from the wine and the thought of talking to Celia. She studied her reflection in the oval mirror that hung in the hallway. She tucked in a wisp of hair that had gotten loose from the rest.

"Hello. How are you?" The familiar voice made Celia smile.

"Wondering when you're going to grace us with your presence. Actually, *we're* wondering. Amanda's called every day."

"Oh, I'm sorry. She's become a perfect nuisance."

"No, she just misses you, and so do I. The ranch just isn't the same without you. In fact, if you don't get here soon Libby and I will probably kill each other."

"Celia . . ."

"Yes," Celia said, her heart dropping to her stomach.

"I want to stay for a while. If it's all right with you."

"Stay with Karen?" Celia said, alarmed.

"No, with you, silly. You know, roomies."

"That sounds wonderful, perfectly wonderful. When are you coming home?"

"Tomorrow, as a matter of fact."

"Good."

That night Celia went to bed thinking, I don't care what this is, but it's better than anything I've had for a while. She's staying, and that's all that matters.


Maggie stood in the hall.

"Let's take a look," Karen said, examining Maggie. She was wearing a pair of long khaki shorts, a pressed white shirt, and a vest of southwestern design. She was sporting a new pair of brown Birkenstocks and a silver ankle bracelet.

"I feel absolutely ridiculous."

"You look absolutely gorgeous. I'd fuck you in a second. Given the chance, of course."

Karen had taken her to Phoenix and shopped for clothes. Karen picked them out, made Maggie model, and then purchased them. There had been protest on all points. But Maggie had to admit that her swarthy companion had good taste. Karen had Maggie's hair cut shoulder-length so that her natural curls became evident, with soft locks encircling her face and green eyes. She looked good. She also looked ten years younger. She was tanned, lean, and well-dressed. In a matter of days, Karen had turned Maggie into a tasteful, dignified, drop-dead gorgeous, femme dyke. Wouldn't Celia be pleased with what Karen had done to her Barbie doll!

"Okay, now it's time to hang with the women folk," Karen said, holding the door.

Maggie looked at her, uncertain.

"C'mon, have some balls. It'll do you good."

* * * * *

When they walked into the bar, Maggie turned
heads. She attributed it to being new in a small town,
but Karen smiled mischievously. They sat at a table
with Sidney and Julia. A young woman was with them.
"This is Emily. You guys just missed her the
other night. She came up with friends from
California," Julia said.

Maggie took the proffered hand. Emily met her
gaze, and her brilliant blue eyes seemed to smile in
welcome. She was slim and muscular, dressed in a
sleeveless shirt and shorts, her light brown hair
twisted into a ponytail.

Karen ordered beers.

"Maggie is staying with our friend Celia as a
summer apprentice in her ceramic studio," Julia told
Emily.

"Sounds like you're going to have an exciting
summer. All women, I take it?" Emily said, looking
at Maggie inquisitively.

Maggie nodded her head in agreement and took a
sip of beer. The music started, and they watched as a
woman sang and played the guitar. She had a good
voice, and her lyrics were what Maggie recognized as
woman-oriented. She drank, laughed, and talked. She
found herself having a really good time. Emily was
especially attentive, and Maggie liked her more with
every passing moment. When Emily asked Maggie to
go outside with her to see her "new favorite place,"
Maggie instantly agreed.

They sneaked out the back door with two fresh
beers. Emily led her down the street to a semi
deserted lot. At the back of the tumbled landscape

was a partially-demolished brick building. There were only three walls and no roof. The moonlight shone on the dusty concrete floor. They sat in an empty window frame and looked out to the illuminated valley.

"Wow," was all Maggie could muster. It was an absolutely breathtaking view.

"Cool, isn't it? I knew you'd like it," Emily said.

"I do."

"Maggie, can I ask you a question?"

"Sure," Maggie said, gazing out into the night.

"Are you and Karen lovers? I didn't think you were, but . . ."

Maggie looked at her, feeling suddenly drunk on everything. "Emily, at this point I'm not entirely convinced that I'm harboring lesbian tendencies. May I ask you a question?"

"Anything," Emily replied.

"How old are you?"

"I'm thirty-four. How old are you?"

"I'm forty-six."

"You don't look it," Emily said.

"Well, thank you."

"Do you feel better now?"

"Knowing that you're thirty-four and not my daughter's age, yes."

"Would it matter?"

"Matter because of what?" Maggie asked nonchalantly.

"Because I'd really like to kiss you."

"Oh." But Maggie's protest was interrupted by Emily's full lips as they pressed against her own. Maggie found her tongue intertwined with another. She could feel the kiss linger and begin again until she was forced to admit she was an active partner. Desire began to stir.

"Emily, now really, this is . . ."

"Shhh, this is really nice," Emily said. She put her finger to Maggie's lips with one hand and undid Maggie's shirt, reaching slowly inside to touch her breast. Maggie closed her eyes. Emily's lips and tongue were on her nipple, bringing it to strident attention. Maggie knew she was lost and didn't care. Men, women, Emily, Celia, whatever, whoever, just somebody fuck me. Maggie succumbed to a collage of physical delights, abandoning herself to Emily's will and whim. Emily reached inside her.

Maggie looked at Emily, meeting her gaze, falling into her eyes. "I don't really know . . ."

"Let me show you," Emily said, taking her hand.

The rest was a blur of sensation. Maggie found herself delighted by a veritable stranger, and it didn't matter. They held each other beneath the moon, dusty from the floor, smiling and sweaty.

Maggie rolled on her back. "Oh, my."

"You're wonderful," Emily said, smiling and kissing her cheek.


Karen stood outside on the sidewalk with Julia and Sidney, all waiting to see if their missing guests would make an appearance. Maggie and Emily strode down the street to meet them.

"Having fun, ladies?" Karen asked, smiling.

"I wanted to show Maggie my favorite place," Emily offered, knowing that Maggie was not up to being publicly grilled.

Maggie smiled at her and thought, I just met you, had sex with you, and now I'm going to find myself missing you.

"Okay, are we calling it an evening?" Sidney asked.

"Yeah, we'll catch up with you in a minute."

Emily caught Maggie's hand. "Don't be scared. I don't expect anything, just that you know it was special, okay?"

Maggie looked at her, relieved yet remorseful. She ran to catch up with Karen.

"Well, my darling, what have we been up to?"

"What do you mean?"

Karen pulled tumbleweed fragments from the back of Maggie's hair and dusted off her shoulders.

"If I didn't know better, I'd say you were fucking around."

Maggie was instantly horrified. "Karen, I can't believe what happened."

Karen laughed. "Celia's gonna kill me."

"Why?"

"Because she'll think I brought you up here to have you seduced."

"Did you?" Maggie asked, smiling from ear to ear.

"No, I had no intention. I just wanted to show you a good time and make Celia realize a few things. I hope you aren't going to tell her what happened."

"I don't know what to do."

"Well, how was it?" Karen laughed. "She was awfully cute."

"Oh my," was all Maggie could muster.

Karen laughed heartily. "This is funny."

\* \* \* \* \*

The next morning Maggie awoke with a throbbing headache and a fire in her stomach. She lay there trying to recreate the evening. Much of it was a blur, which worried her.

Karen found her lying on the couch with a cold, wet washcloth covering her eyes and forehead.

"Not feeling so well this morning?" Karen inquired.

"I don't want to talk about it."

"I bet, you drunken convert."

Maggie removed the washcloth and sat up on her elbow. "What does it mean? Am I a lesbian now? I still can't believe I did it. How am I going to face Celia? She'll think I'm horrid." She lay back and groaned. "It's a horrible mess."

"Will you relax? I'll take you home tomorrow when you feel better."

"No, I told Celia I'd be home today. She's expecting me."

"Not in this particular condition."

"Karen, you've got to help me. What am I going to do?"

"If I were you, I'd keep this our little secret. Why does she really need to know? It's not like you two are married or anything. You didn't commit adultery, Maggie. You're an unattached woman who can do what she so desires. And if you desire to roll around in a deserted building in the middle of the night with a sex kitten, it's your affair," Karen said, laughing.

"You're not being very sympathetic."

"No, actually I'm jealous. Baby dyke scores."

"Is that what I am?"

"You're Maggie. C'mon. I'll make you a surefire

hangover-helper breakfast. I can't return you as damaged goods."

"Technically speaking, I am."

"Maggie, take it for what it is, a beautiful experience. You don't have to worry or wonder anymore. You now know. Let it go at that."


The "surefire" breakfast didn't work. Karen had to stop the car twice for Maggie to throw up.

When Karen pulled up in front of the house, Maggie was reclined with a wet handkerchief over her forehead. They couldn't have chosen a worse moment. Celia and Libby were on the front porch with two apprentices who had flown in early that morning. Celia came toward them, smiling. Karen got out of the car and said something charming to the audience. Maggie opened the car door and threw up.

Celia looked horrified. "What did you do to her?"

"I think we had a little too much fun last night."

"Christ, Karen."

"Sorry. I'm not always the best guardian."

Karen and Celia helped Maggie out of the car. Maggie looked at Celia and smiled weakly. They led her past the other women, and Maggie waved a hand in welcome. Celia put her to bed.


Karen was in the kitchen having a glass of lemonade.

"Who are the youngsters?"

"The new apprentices."

"I'm sorry about Maggie. I wanted to keep her an extra day until she felt better, but she insisted on coming. I think it was the car ride."

"You shouldn't have let her drink so much."

"I didn't realize she had, but she did have a really good time. Got some things out of her system."

"What's that supposed to mean?"

"Our little Maggie isn't so little anymore."

"I suppose you seduced her, too," Celia said flippantly.

"No, I didn't do that."

Celia looked astounded. "Tell me you didn't hire someone . . ."

"I would never," Karen said, smiling. "Okay, I've got to go. I'd love to stay and chat. Tell Maggie to call me."


It was dark when Maggie awoke. After she had a bath and brushed her teeth, she felt human again — and hungry. She went down to the kitchen hoping to be alone. She wasn't up to facing anyone after having made such an ass out of herself. Celia was sitting at the kitchen bar reading.

"Feeling better?"

"Much. I'm sorry. I'm so embarrassed."

"Don't be. Come here," Celia said, extending her arms. Maggie fell into them gratefully, feeling safe. Celia brushed her hair back from her face.

"You look different."

Maggie was instantly embarrassed. "Different? How?"

"Did you get a haircut?"

"Oh, that! Yes. Karen decided I needed some sprucing up."

"So you got a haircut."

"I also have a new wardrobe with a 'funk edge' to it, according to Karen."

"Anything else new?"

Maggie turned to the fridge and began searching its contents. "No, not really. Why do you ask?" She knows or at least wonders. This is awful.

"Just curious. I'm glad you're back. I don't care what happened."

"What could possibly have happened?"

"You tell me."

"There's nothing to tell."

"So what did you do up there?"

"Went out for every conceivable meal, visited everyone in town, went out for drinks."

"Did you meet some new friends?"

"Yes, I did. Celia, if I didn't know better, I'd think you were grilling me."

"Karen just worries me. I mean she's not what I would call a good influence."

"Celia, I'm a grown woman and I can take care of myself. Karen isn't responsible for my bad behavior."

"What kind of bad behavior?"

Maggie looked at her, flushed and angry. "I don't have to explain myself to anyone." She took her sandwich upstairs, leaving Celia sitting there stunned.

Maggie stopped midway up the stairs. "But since you're so inquisitive, if you really want to know, I got drunk and got laid."

Celia burst into tears. Maggie closed the door to

her room with force. She set her sandwich on the nightstand. I shouldn't have done that. That was mean.

Celia took all the beer bottles she could find in the fridge and carried them outside to the pool. She sat in the chaise lounge and began to get methodically drunk.

She awoke to the sound of someone tripping over a beer bottle. It rolled toward the pool. She heard the splash, and then voices. When she opened her eyes it was bright, and three faces peered down at her, Maggie, Libby, and one of the new apprentices, Olivia. Anna had the good taste to stay behind in the kitchen, flipping the pancakes Libby had begun before they went to investigate.

"What the fuck are you doing? First it's Maggie, and now you. Maybe we should just send both of you off to the Betty Ford Clinic, get you cleaned up, and then maybe we can get back to the business at hand," Libby said.

"Are you all right?" Maggie asked, feeling guilty.

"I don't have to explain myself to anyone. I am, after all, a grown woman," Celia replied.

"I'm sorry, Celia. That was mean. I didn't want you to find out that way. It just came out."

"It figures you'd be behind this," Libby said snidely.

"Libby, you'd better shut that nasty mouth of yours before I do it for you," Maggie said.

"That I would like to see," Libby said.

Maggie took a step closer and pushed Libby. "Don't fuck with me, Libby. I mean it."

"Go fuck yourself!" Libby said, pushing her back.

Maggie pushed her again, hard. Libby grabbed her wrist. Maggie pulled free. Olivia stepped in between them.

"C'mon, ladies. Let's not do this."

"Not until she learns to shut her mouth," Maggie said, flushed with anger.

"Maggie, Libby, stop it right now!" Celia ordered.

Maggie stepped back, still glaring at Libby.

"That's right, listen to Mama," Libby chided.

That was too much for Maggie. She charged, pushing Libby with enough force to send her flying into the pool. Libby came up sputtering and ready to kill. Olivia grabbed Libby, and Celia followed up. They both held Libby as she inched them toward Maggie.

Celia looked at Maggie. "Go inside right now, dammit!"

In her rush, Maggie almost knocked Anna flat as she stood in the doorway. She flew upstairs to her room and locked the door. She sat on her bed, shaking. Someone knocked on the door.

"Maggie?"

Maggie got up and unlocked the door. She looked at Celia sheepishly.

"I'm sorry," Maggie said. That was really uncalled for. I don't know how I'm going to face those women. They must think I'm a drunken brawler."

"Between the two of us, we're not making a good impression. At least this way they know that getting older doesn't mean getting dull," Celia said, laughing.

"Is Libby all right?"

"Of course. A little shaken, perhaps."

"I can't believe I did that."

"C'mon, on let's have breakfast. I sent Libby into town, so the coast is clear."

\* \* \* \* \*

"Celia?"

"Yes?"

"I'm sorry about how I treated you last night. I'm having trouble processing what's going on in my life, and I'm a little sensitive."

"So how was he?"

Maggie looked at her, surprised. "It wasn't a man."

Celia dropped her coffee cup. Black liquid seeped across the white tile floor; the cup was in several pieces, some of them still spinning. Anna turned to look at both of them.

"You guys are a queer bunch."

They burst out laughing.


When Libby returned, she opted not to speak to Maggie the rest of the day. The ranch was large enough that one could steer clear of the other. Maggie spent the day working in the now burgeoning garden. Celia came out with a pitcher of lemonade and two glasses.

"How's it going in there?" Maggie asked, indicating the studio.

"I think Anna and Olivia are going to work out well. They seem to like it here so far, despite certain events."

"Christ. I used to be so well-mannered."

"I wouldn't worry about it. Olivia has already been filling us in on other summers spent with women. This isn't new."

"I don't know if I should be relieved or concerned."

"Are you all right?"

"What do you mean?"

"With what happened up there?"

"Oh, that. Yeah, I think so."

"How did it happen? If you don't want to talk about it, I'd understand."

"Actually, I'm kind of embarrassed. I've never done anything like it. We rolled around on a dusty concrete floor under the moonlight."

"Moonlight is good," Celia said, smiling to cover a tinge of jealousy. Part of her was relieved it wasn't a man. She'd spent last night thinking she'd lost Maggie to the world of men, a place she couldn't go.

"Celia, I don't know why it happened. I'm glad that it did, but I never meant to hurt you in the process."

"You didn't do anything Maggie. I was pushing you, and I got what I deserved."

"No, you didn't deserve that. I was going to tell you. I was just scared."

"Why?"

"For starters, it was slightly out of character."

"You're not the first woman to have this experience later in life."

"I know. I'm just glad it's over, that I experienced it. Now I know about things that I've wondered about."

"So what do you think?"

"I don't think I've ever quite felt that way before. It was nice."

"You liked it?" Celia asked, feeling herself blush slightly and hoping Maggie wouldn't notice.

"Very much. If you ever get around to seducing me, you won't be my first."

Celia was stunned. "Maggie!"

"I know you respect me too much. You better go. Libby is tapping her fingers. Some pressing business matter, I'm sure," Maggie said, watching Libby approach.

Celia walked off in a daze.


"You know what I think?" Olivia said, rolling out another slab.

"Do tell," Anna said, smiling. She was getting used to Olivia's speculations on other people's lives. They had been friends, lovers, and then friends for the past five years.

"I think Celia and Maggie are in love. They're just not willing to admit to it, not yet at least."

"And if you have anything to do with it, that will soon be remedied," said Anna.

"Exactly. They simply need a little prodding."

"What about Libby? She made it more than obvious that Celia was her property. Hands off and all that."

"I think she's running scared. If you're secure you don't need announcements."

"True."

"Besides, Libby's a nasty little wench. Wait till you get to ride to town with her. It's not my idea of fun. She's fucked up."

"Maggie's pretty," Anna said.

"And Celia's hot."

"They'd make a good couple, but Cupid isn't always reliable."

"Meaning?" Olivia asked.

"There's a pretty good chance they won't get together. One of them has got to make a move, and both of them have a lot of baggage."

"With a little help we could change that."

"What are you suggesting, pushing them into a small space and not letting them go until they make mutual protestations?"

"Something like that," Olivia declared.

"You make me nervous when you do that," Anna said.

"I'm simply acting as an embassy for the goddess."

"No, you're playing matchmaker."

"Aren't you going to say that by doing so I fulfill my own aching need to find companionship?" Olivia added, her blue eyes flashing.

"Exactly," Anna replied.

"You know me so well. It's a pity we make better friends than lovers."

"What makes you so sure about that?" Anna asked.

"Past history has not been kind to us."

"People think we're weird, you know, because we hang out and can't seem to make up our minds," Anna replied, shrugging her shoulders.

"So what? I can't help it that you're my best friend."

"Maybe that's what Maggie and Celia are feeling," Anna said, disappearing into a maze of shelves.

"Damn, I hate when you do that," Olivia said.

"Do what?"

"Draw some insightful parallel and leave me to decipher it alone."

"That is, after all, the purpose, dear."

# Chapter Five

"She's in love with you, you know," Karen said to Celia's back. They had finished their business dealings, and Karen was in a mood to probe. She had seen how Maggie looked at Celia, and she'd seen Celia look back.

Celia was watching Maggie work through the large studio window. The jars of glaze on the shelves behind made her look like a madonna in a stained-glass piece.

Celia turned around. "What did you say?"

"I said she's in love with you."

"Who?"

"Maggie. Who else? She won't have Emily because she's got her heart set on you."

"Emily?"

"The other half of rolling about on a dusty floor in the moonlight."

"I thought it was a one-night stand."

Karen produced a postcard. "One of many."

"Really?"

"Maggie has been less than candid. She doesn't want to hurt Emily's feelings. If you ask me, it was a case of person as instrument. Unfortunately, Emily appears quite infatuated. Maggie's gonna have to fess up but she doesn't know how to do it."

"Maybe you could help her with that."

"No, I think you should just tell her that you'd like to be more than friends," Karen said, taking Celia by the shoulders and shaking them.

"It would ruin our friendship."

"Why?"

"Because neither one of us is strong enough. Because if it was meant to be, it would have happened years ago."

"What are you afraid of?"

Celia turned to look at her. "Nothing."

"Tell me the truth."

"I don't know what's true anymore."

"You do. Tell me."

Celia studied Karen's face, measuring the risk.

"You'll tell her," she said flatly.

"I won't. I only pass gossip that doesn't count. I swear," Karen said, holding up two fingers. "Girl Scout's honor."

"I was a Girl Scout once."

"In the heart of every Girl Scout lurks a dyke."

"Karen . . ."

"You're in love, aren't you?"

Celia confessed. "I'm scared. I can feel myself falling in love. And I see her leaving when she's through dabbling in social anarchy. I can't bear that, Karen. So let it be. That's just the way it is."

"Celia, you're a fool if you let her go."

"Then I'm a fool," Celia said with conviction. I won't succumb, she thought. I won't walk into her life and take what I have no right to. I hurt her once. I can't do it again.

"I haven't given her any of the postcards Emily's sent," Karen said.

"Give them to her. The property of the post is the person's to whom it's addressed."

"Yeah, right."


Maggie watched Celia walk off into the desert and took the stack of postcards from her pocket. She spread them out in front of her, face up, studying their shiny fronts. San Francisco looked beautiful. She'd never been there. Harold had refused. Too many homosexuals. The passing years had never removed the sour taste from his mouth.

"Have you ever been to California?" Olivia asked coming up behind her.

"No."

"You should. So who's the admirer?"

"What admirer?"

94

"I've been accused of many things, but stupid is not one of them."

"Her name is Emily. I met her in Jerome."

"And?"

"And we rolled around together and it was wonderful, but not anything I'm capable of sustaining. I really wish she hadn't sent these."

"Because you love Celia."

Maggie looked at the postcards. What is this thing called love? She had been fond of Harold, but it wasn't love. She wanted to be with Celia, whatever that meant, but if they hadn't got together by now, how could she expect them to later?

"Olivia, let it be."

"Why?"

"Because I said so. Do you have a match?"

"Yeah."

"May I have one please?" Maggie said, scooping up the postcards.

"Only if you promise to tell me what you really feel."

They watched the pile burn in the small pit they had dug.

"What did she want?" Olivia asked.

"Who?"

"Emily."

"I don't know. I didn't read them."

"Why not?"

"Because it can't be. Why add to the pile of justifications I already have going?"

"What are you justifying?"

"My own incredible inertia."

"Why inert?"

"Why not?"

Olivia's eyes got big, and her face was serious. "Because it's the biggest waste of your life, of your heart. Don't do it, Maggie."

"There's nothing to do. Olivia, I appreciate your concern, but it's not possible to have everything on one's wish list. Life's not like that."

Maggie stamped out the fire and buried the ashes with the edge of her boot. She shrugged her shoulders at Olivia and walked off without saying another word.


Olivia became obsessed with trying to figure out how to get the two women together.

"If it doesn't happen, then it wasn't meant to be. They're grown-ups, Olivia. They know what to do if they want it."

"That's not true, Anna. I bet they've never even talked about how they feel."

"And you think you can make that happen?"

"Possibly."

"Good luck."


Celia leaned on the kitchen counter, watching Maggie and Olivia head off in the direction of the arroyo. She mused on the outline of their bodies against the pink and orange of the desert sky. Their easy-stepping profiles seemed appreciative of the feeling a good day of hard work brings to a body. One's breath in the stillness, the hard dirt beneath the feet, the slow buzzing of the cicadas as they strike up their electric orchestra.

She turned to see Libby scowling at them. It was no surprise Celia and Libby didn't make good lovers. They didn't like the same things. Libby was miserable, and Celia knew that Libby honestly did not know why. No amount of loving was going to rid her of it.

"I don't know why you let them go off like that when there are still things to be done."

"Watching the sun go down in the desert is one of them," Celia said, smiling.

"I hardly think so."

"Libby, you're the only one to have passed through here and remained totally untouched by the beauty and serenity. Peace is to be found here. Don't you want to experience some of that?"

"I came here to learn, not fawn over the local flora."

Celia looked at her, sadness clouding her eyes. You can't save her, only she can do that. But first she must know she is dying slowly each day without ever having lived. Celia put her arm around Libby's shoulders.

"I wish I could show you the desert through my eyes, teach you to love it like I do."

Libby looked into Celia's eyes, her own becoming cloudy and filling with tears. Celia wiped them away.

"Why don't you try? Show me. Help me to see."

Celia held her. "I don't mean to hurt you, Libby."

"Then why do you?" Libby asked between sobs.

"Because I'm a selfish woman who isn't ready for another failure. Because I know I can't make you happy."

"You don't even try," Libby said, breaking away.

That night Celia took Libby to bed, only this time they didn't make love. They talked. And they held each other, a mother holding her lost daughter.


In the morning Celia turned away from Maggie, feeling torn and confused. She wanted to be alone again so she could find herself. She felt the edges of depression closing in. Her sanctuary was turning against her.

Celia knew what she should do, but she couldn't muster the energy or courage to do it. I am a coward. I should tell Libby that no amount of emotional coercion can keep me, that it's over, that love out of pity isn't the right kind of love. Then I should march up to Maggie and say, Look. I don't know how you feel, but I love you and want you. And if that isn't what you want, please tell me so I can stop wishing for things that will never be.

Instead, she found herself in the office, sobbing. She heard Anna, Olivia, and Maggie come in the kitchen door. She wiped her eyes, shuffled some papers, and tried to avoid looking at Maggie when she walked in.

"Are you all right?"

"I'm fine."

"No, you're not. You've been crying," Maggie replied.

"I have."

"Why?"

"I feel lost sometimes."

"Is it something I've done? It's not the postcards or anything, is it?"

"No, it's not that. That's your affair."

"No, it's not anything like that."

"I know, Maggie, I didn't mean anything by it. I'm just having a bad day."

"Is it Libby?" Maggie asked.

"That's part of it."

"And you don't want to talk about the other part, right?"

"Right."

"If you want to talk ..."

"I know."

Maggie walked off. Pangs of hurt and jealousy tore at the corners of her heart. She was jealous that Celia had spent the night with Libby. She knew she had no right to feel that way, but she couldn't help it.


Maggie and Olivia sat by the stream dangling their feet in the cool, clear water.

"How do you feel about having slept with a woman? You were married once, right?"

"What is your obsession with my love life?"

"I care about you. You're my friend, and I want to help."

Maggie looked at her blue-eyed friend, deciding.

"Talk about it, Maggie. It will make you feel better."

"All right, I'm scared. I still find it strange."

"Why strange?"

"It feels odd to have experienced a lesbian relationship now. Why not twenty years ago? I've spent most of my adult life being straight, and now this. It's confusing."

"Maggie, have you ever heard of compulsory heterosexuality?"

"No."

"Well, basically it means that we are all taught from the moment we're born to be straight. Everything is laid out, and we simply follow it."

"Do you mean I could have been a lesbian all along and never known it?"

"It's highly possible and would certainly explain what you're feeling. You've never been in this environment before, but once in it you are simply responding to your natural instincts."

"I feel stupid, like I should have known a long time ago that I was different."

"You are who you are now, and that's all that matters. So fess up. Are you in love with Celia?"

"Am I that obvious?"

"You both are. Why do you think it twists Libby's shorts so?"

"Is it foolishness on our parts?"

"It's only foolishness when you deny that it's real. If you love Celia, let her know."

"How do I that? Walk up and say, Hey, I've been meaning to tell you something?"

"Or you could just look her in the eyes, kiss her, and go from there."

"Seduce her?"

"Exactly."

"I don't know about that."

"Maggie, you're going to have to be the one to make the move. Celia won't do it. She's afraid — more afraid than you are. It's up to you, Maggie. Be the strong one."

"What about Libby?"

"Fuck her. She's just a passing fancy. Don't give up a life of happiness for a surly bitch who hangs on for selfish reasons."

Maggie lay on the Navajo rug with her legs in the air, trying to stretch the ache from the small of her back. She had spent the afternoon kneading clay and listening to Olivia and Anna recount psycho-bitch stories after she had been silly enough to ask what psycho-bitches were.

"Tell her, Anna," Olivia said.

Anna smiled her quirky smile. She was the embodiment of an imp. She was short, stout, strong, and tanned like the rest of them. Her round face took on a mischievous air; her hazel eyes sparkled. Anna was a storyteller.

"They are girlfriends that make your life hell. They scream at you for everything. They're control freaks. You can't please them. What works one day will get you hanged the next. They flirt and tease one minute and slap you five seconds later. They are the Tasmanian devils of love. They make you wonder why you love them, and when you threaten to leave they instantly become the seductive sweet woman that made you love them in the first place. But two hours later, after seriously fucking your brains out, they revert. It's awful, and a prime example would be Libby. Watch her, and you'll know exactly what we mean."

"Well, I'll definitely steer clear of them."

"What do you mean? You attempted to drown one of them," Olivia said, smiling.

"I did not."

"Whatever you say."


Maggie was still embarrassed about throwing Libby in the pool. She had apologized to Libby, and they had gone on tolerating each other. Maggie was secretly relieved the other two apprentices, Kate and Madeline, had not yet arrived to see anything. It was bad enough putting up with Olivia's teasing.

They all teased one another, and only Libby found it offensive. Libby hated Olivia, and now with Kate and Madeline delivering quips whenever they got the chance she was pushed beyond her boiling point.

Olivia, of course, was the ringleader, and Maggie was a willing foot soldier. They had all been called into Celia's office for a counseling session at least once.

"You called her a tit-head?" Celia asked, sitting on the corner of her desk as she seriously considered her friend.

Maggie stood at attention, ready for the court-martial.

"You make me feel like I'm twelve years old."

"At the moment, you are. Now please tell me what is going on. This is not how it's supposed to be. We're supposed to be women in harmony with one another, working together."

"Well, Libby's the stick in the smooth-running cog. She may be in charge, but her leadership skills are definitely lacking. She has it in for Olivia, and she consistently assigns her the worst chores. It's not fair. I told her so, and in the process called her a tit-head."

"That was before you threatened to drop the piece she's labored over for the last two weeks."

"All right, I admit that was extreme, but she taunts me. She asked me what I was going to do about it. I was driven to a demonstration."

Celia rubbed her temples. "Maggie, please. I need your help. I know she's difficult, but all of you banded together is not fair."

"The woman is a fiend," Maggie said, sticking her hands in the back pockets of her clay-covered shorts.

"She needs some understanding."

"And we'd give it if she wasn't so nasty. She doesn't want any of us here. She's made that more than evident."

"Maggie."

"All right. For you I will try to refrain from acts of violence, but being nice depends on her."

"Thank you."

Maggie walked to where Celia stood by the window and brushed the stray hairs from Celia's shoulders.

"I don't mean to be difficult. I've been so well-mannered for so long. I've buried things I shouldn't have, held my tongue when I wanted to scream. Now I feel free, and saying what's on my mind is part of it. I'll try to be more compassionate, but I won't let Libby walk over me or my friends," Maggie said, looking deeply into Celia's eyes.

They both tried to read the other's unspoken words. Celia broke away, looking out the window. She wished she could tell her friend all the things she felt, but she hadn't the courage.

Celia found Maggie on the rug.

"You know, for an old gal you sure have nice legs," Celia said.

Maggie opened her eyes and looked at them. "You really think so?"

"Yes. Practicing a little yoga?"

"Trying to stretch my back. It hurts."

"You were on kneading detail today. Takes a lot out of a person."

"I thought I was getting stronger, but after this afternoon I'm not so sure."

"You are getting stronger," Celia said, sitting down next to her, taking an arm and rubbing it.

"That feels good," Maggie said, closing her eyes and arching her neck to feel Celia's closeness. Maggie missed being close to Celia. But ever since she had crossed over the line, both women guarded themselves, afraid to be too close. They no longer joked using sexual innuendos, which might mean something. Right now, none of that mattered. Now they were content to be in each other's presence, whatever that meant.

"Want a back rub?"

"Sure."

"Come on then."

"Where are we going?"

"The kitchen counter doubles as a massage table."

"You're not serious."

"I am," Celia replied, taking a bottle of lavender oil from the cupboard.

"What's that?"

"Oil. Take off your shirt," Celia commanded, spreading a white sheet across the countertop.

"You're serious about this."

"Yes. I took classes, as a matter of fact."

"So you know what you're doing?"

"You'll find out. Shirt off and up on the table. Normally it's a naked affair, but this is close enough," Celia said, pulling at the hem of Maggie's skimpy running shorts.

"And we are in the kitchen after all."

"Exactly."

Maggie lay on the smooth sheet, her body covered lightly in oil, listening to the soothing sounds of Joni Mitchell on the stereo. Outside, afternoon was fading into twilight.

"Try to relax," Celia commanded, working the tenseness out of Maggie's shoulders. "This is supposed to remove stress, not create it."

"I'm on the kitchen counter half-naked."

"They're only breasts, Maggie. I'm sure we've all seen them before."

"But they're my breasts."

"And they're lovely. But for practical purposes, they're not showing, so relax."

"You say *relax* just like the gynecologist."

"I promise I won't put spoons up your crotch," Celia said as she generously spread oil on Maggie's back and legs. She began by rubbing the arches of Maggie's feet, slowly, smoothly. Her even strokes relieved the tenseness Maggie had built up. Beneath Celia's insistent skill she forgot her discomfort. Her body began to respond to her friend's touch.

Celia gently stroked Maggie's inner thigh, kneading the muscle, running her hand back and forth. Maggie opened her eyes and looked up at Celia who had her eyes closed, going by feel, her face flushed. Maggie felt her own body growing warm. Celia placed her hands at the small of Maggie's back at the site of the pain. Maggie cried out, and Celia continued to ease the tight knots in Maggie's back and thighs.

Maggie's mind began to wander as relaxation and a sense of calm flooded her senses. She breathed the lavender that enveloped her body. She watched the shadow of the oleander bush as it swayed and danced upon the blind. She found herself floating into a sea of unspent emotion, of wanting and needing things.

Celia worked the muscles of Maggie's forearms and hands, slowly rubbing each finger and palm, in strong, even strokes.

"You have strong arms," Celia said. It was nice to touch Maggie's body, but remaining impartial was becoming increasingly difficult. It became impossible when Maggie sat up. Her nakedness made Celia flush as her eyes caressed Maggie's face, trying to read what was written there.

"Strong enough to hold you?" Maggie asked, wrapping her arms around Celia's neck and pulling her close to kiss her. Lips melting into one, tongues embracing, quivering, dancing, daring to say what eyes only hinted at. When it was over Celia looked deep into Maggie's eyes.

"You'd better watch it. You'll get more than you bargained for with that, little lady," Celia said nervously.

"Maybe I want more," Maggie said and kissed her again.

Celia's resistance and caution suddenly became things of the past. She succumbed to all she was feeling. If it meant punishment and remorse tomorrow then so be it, but right now she wanted that woman. Celia buried her face in Maggie's breasts. Tears formed, and she tasted the salt mingled with Maggie's soft brown nipples. Touch, taste, smell enveloped Celia until she was totally lost in Maggie's body.

Her happy revelry was interrupted by the slam of the screen door. Celia turned. Celia and Maggie met Libby's departing gaze. Not a word was spoken; everything had been said. Celia started to pull away. Maggie panicked.

"You can't leave me now."

Celia knew where she had to be. She held Maggie. Both women cried, laughing, kissing, caressing. Maggie removed Celia's shirt, feeling each pearl button as she unfastened it, slipping her hand past the rough denim to the silky smoothness of the breast beneath. Maggie thought she would collapse in ecstasy. Celia kissed Maggie's thighs, nestling in their warm firmness. She looked up.

Maggie stroked Celia's hair, then her cheek, and said, "Take me to bed." Her voice was throaty and deep, and Celia had no doubt she meant it.

And Celia did, letting Maggie undress and touch each part of her quivering body. Maggie marveled at each electric touch. Celia pulled her close, and Maggie felt the heat of Celia's tongue between her legs, the smoothness of her tongue gliding between the pink folds, the ease of Celia's fingers as they slipped inside.

Maggie felt herself rocking, thrusting, crying out for more, her hips spread far apart. Then the quiver, the arrow to her core, an explosion of nerves, tendons and sinews stretched to the breaking point. She lay back in a spasm of uncontrollable glee.

Celia and Maggie didn't speak. They each took the other over and over again until satiated. At last, they fell into a deep sleep, not caring what the morrow would bring.


Celia found Maggie standing and staring at the crumpled sheet in the middle of the bed. It looked deserted in the midst of love.

Maggie turned to her. "It looks so forlorn."

Celia picked up the sheet and wrapped it around Maggie's shoulders. "There, does the percale feel loved again?"

"Yes," Maggie said, happily pulling Celia to her and kissing her.

"Come shower with me," Celia said, feeling her loins turning to butter again. The two women couldn't seem to get enough of each other. Their minds, bodies, tongues, hearts crying out to hold, touch, love.

They were noticeably late for breakfast. The

apprentices, knowing something had happened, watched them descend the tile staircase. Olivia suppressed an overwhelming desire to clap, to stand in enthusiastic congratulation to two people who had come to such pleasant terms with their desire.

Later in the studio, Olivia was still thinking about it. "It's like a happy ending. Everyone gets what she wants."

Anna looked at her friend and then out the window. "Not everyone."

Olivia moved to the window. "Oh, yeah, the nazi queen gets the shaft. She wasn't good for Celia, and we don't live in a perfect world. It's still a happy ending in my book."

"Celia and Maggie have a lot of trials and troubles ahead of them."

"You're such a pessimist sometimes," Olivia said grimly. They watched Celia talking to Libby, who was throwing various personal possessions in the back of her truck. Celia stood with her hands in her pockets, helpless.

"I wouldn't want to be in Celia's shoes right now," Anna said.

"Me either," Olivia replied.

"You could have at least told me so I didn't have to find out like that. How can you be so cruel? Did you have to fuck each other in the kitchen? Couldn't you have a little more discretion? Why didn't you tell me you were in love with her?" Libby was screaming now. The apprentices looked at one another and pretended not to hear.

Maggie walked off in the direction of the arroyo. The situation was uncomfortable, and she didn't want to bear witness. Part of her felt bad for Libby, but a deeper part knew her life would not be complete without Celia. She had waited much too long to be chivalrous to Libby's passing obsession. Libby would find someone else; there was no one else for Maggie. She threw a stick into the arroyo, listened to it hit the rock walls, lay on her back, ran her fingers through the hot sand, and looked up at the perfect blue sky. I'm in love and it's wonderful. Absolutely wonderful.

Meanwhile, outside the studio, things had gotten ugly. Libby, unable to elicit any more response from Celia than "I'm sorry," had taken things from the back of the truck and begun throwing them in Celia's direction. The apprentices were forced to intervene. Olivia and Anna put Libby in the cab while the other two reloaded the truck.

"Come on, Libby, let her go. She doesn't love you, and it's best to just leave," Olivia advised.

Libby finally shrugged her shoulders and sped off, leaving a cloud of dust in her wake.

Celia watched from the safety of the porch. The sky was turning pink, and the cloud banks were building. An electric smell announced the oncoming storm. Rainstorm season. The calm before the storm, Celia thought.

Celia saw the silhouette of the woman she loved coming toward her across the horizon. Her heart beat faster, and desire swelled in her veins. Maggie approached slowly. She felt guilty for being happy at the cost of Libby's misery. But she felt worse for Celia for having to take the brunt of it.

Celia walked toward her, took her hand, held her. "It's over. Finally over. I'm sorry you had to be part of it."

Maggie smiled and kissed her.

So this is desire, Maggie thought, as she lay naked on her stomach in bed, reading while Celia caressed her rear end.

"My, you have a nice tush for an old broad," Celia said.

"You really think so?" Maggie replied, tossing the book off the bed and taking Celia in her arms.

It was almost embarrassing at times, the way Maggie felt, anywhere and everywhere, when she thought of Celia. She would be creating a pot on the wheel, her concentration focused entirely on the brown clay in front of her, and the next moment she would be thinking about Celia's soft breasts, about making a round brown nipple hard when she took it in her mouth, about Celia's soft noises as Maggie caressed her body.

Sometimes she found herself blushing from these thoughts and was embarrassed when she saw Celia. But Celia, it seemed, had similar thoughts. Celia and Maggie didn't last long in the same room before they came together, first kissing, then holding, then . . .

The afternoon in the arroyo was the worst. They had gone for a walk to sketch the petroglyphs. They had the best of intentions. Yes, they had brought a blanket, but it was only to sit on. One thing led to another until they forgot all about sketching and thought only about each other. When they were through, lying sweating and hot in each other's arms, their uneven breathing in perfect unison, they heard clapping. Looking up they saw Olivia and Anna. Celia told them to scat. Maggie was mortified.

"I doubt they were there long, and we are making love in a public place. Besides, my flirtatious beauty, maybe they learned a thing or two."

"I doubt it. I'm far from experienced."

Celia rolled on her back and looked up at the sky. "But oh, my dear, you know 'nothing' ever so well."

Olivia and Anna must have made a pact never to say anything to Maggie about what they had seen. Still, they looked at her differently. For the first time in her life, Maggie was a verifiable sexual creature. Everything felt so new, so soft, so sensual and so intensified, like time spent under the influence of LSD. She felt high. Then like any addict she began to fear the fall, the day reality would leak in to spoil the party. She feared the day Celia would tire of her, find out she wasn't so special, and grow bored with the whole thing. Sometimes she would cry when Celia made love to her.

"Why do you cry?" Celia asked, trying to kiss the tears away as fast as they were falling. The only reasonable answer Maggie could give was that she was happy and dreaded the day she was made unhappy.

"I solemnly swear to do my damnedest to never make you unhappy — occasionally peeved, but never miserable. All right?"

"All right," Maggie conceded, putting her worry behind her for that day.


Celia sat at the kitchen table, tracing the grain of the wood with her fingertip and listening carefully to Maggie's half of the conversation. Celia knew they must resolve the other part of Maggie's life. They had put off the future, happy simply to enjoy their holiday together. Amanda's calling reminded them that Maggie had loose ends that needed tending.

"I know, Amanda. I am coming home. I'm just not sure when."

Pause. "I know."

Pause. "I know."

Pause. "I am well aware of the fact that I'm a grown woman, have been for years. But I'm not running away from anything. I'm simply enjoying my summer vacation."

Pause. "I know."

Pause. "Look, Amanda, your life is no longer dependent on mine. You don't need me. I'm not rooted to that house. I appreciate your looking after it. Hell, move into it if you want. It's a house, not a living thing, whereas *I* am, and I need some things I'm finding here. Right now I'm not ready to give that up." Maggie refrained from saying, So piss off, but it was an effort.

"I'm hanging up now, Amanda," Maggie said,

waiting a few seconds before placing the phone in its cradle. They both heard Amanda's screeching on the other end. Maggie stood, with her hand still on the phone, staring out at the garden and the desert beyond it. Going home was an unpleasant thought.

"I hate that stupid green hedge, deciduous trees, and lawns."

"What are you talking about?"

"My backyard. Amanda wants me back."

"So I gathered. Are you going?" Celia asked, feeling a lump forming in her throat.

Maggie turned to look at her. "Do you want me to?"

"No. But I can't expect you to stay forever if you think you need to go back."

"That's an easy way to let me down. Make it my doing."

"What do you mean?" Celia asked, genuinely puzzled.

"Like you don't know. Like Libby and the others when you grew tired of them. Summer vacation is over. Time to move on."

"You can't possibly believe that," Celia said, hurt beginning to well up inside.

"I'm not sure about anything anymore," Maggie said, tears springing to her eyes. She didn't want to go, but she couldn't stay without an invitation.

Celia was stricken. Didn't Maggie know how much, how deeply, she loved her? How she had begun to plan her life around her?

"Maggie, I want us to be together, to live together, get old together. I don't want you to leave. Ever. Dammit, I love you."

Maggie turned back around. "I love you too."

"Stay. Please say you'll stay."

"Who said anything about going anywhere?" Maggie said, smiling through watery eyes and sniffing.

"Amanda."

"We'll figure something out. Okay?"

"Promise."

"Girl Scout's honor."

"If I remember correctly, you were thrown out of the troop for threatening anarchy."

"I was young and dangerous."

"And what are you now?"

"Old and crafty."

# Chapter Six

"What are you going to do?" Celia asked.

"You can't possibly expect me to answer that when I'm like this. Celia, you're not being fair," Maggie replied as she straddled Celia's stomach, her hips rocking gently, Celia's fingers inside. She was on the verge of orgasm.

"There is no better time than this. It's hard to lie when you can barely think."

"I wouldn't lie to you."

"Tell me what you want to do." Celia withdrew her fingers.

"Celia, don't stop, please," Maggie begged.

"Answer the question."

"I'll sell the house and live with you forever. How's that?" Maggie felt Celia's fingers back inside.

"Good answer. Now come here," Celia said, pulling Maggie up and kissing the lovely pink folds of her sex.

Celia was relieved. She desperately had hoped that Maggie would give up her Midwestern life and take up residence. Celia had been afraid that family, friends, and property might prevent her.

Maggie knew that the fulfillment of a wish-list promise should never willingly be given up; rather it should be clutched tight. Amanda and the others would simply have to accept the changes in her life. Maggie had been congenial too long. She had come into her own, and she wasn't going back.

It was the middle of another hot August afternoon. Maggie, Olivia, and Anna were refining and remixing a giant mound of brownish-red, slippery mud that would soon become usable clay. They kept adding powdered clay from twenty-pound bags, mixing it into the gooey brown mess, and treading it into large circles with their feet.

"I feel like a Greek making wine, treading all the grapes into a pulpy mess," Maggie said, laughing and wiping beads of sweat from her forehead with the sleeve of her dirty T-shirt and leaving a long smudge of brown dirt behind.

"Only this is thicker, wetter, and heavier," Olivia said. "I can't believe I actually volunteered for this."

"It's part of the process. We can't be so wasteful. It's recycling," Anna said.

"She's a great recycler," Olivia said, "A dedicated type. God forbid if you throw something away that should be put in the recycling bin."

"I'm not that bad."

"You are, but it is an admirable trait," Olivia said, pulling her foot out of the sludge and wiping her brow.

"Besides, the worst part is that it's hot," Anna said, taking off her shirt to reveal her braless front.

"Nice neckline. Doesn't she have bodacious ta ta's?" Olivia said to Maggie.

"What are those?" Maggie asked, sensing the reply.

"Her tits, silly."

"Oh," Maggie replied.

"Come on."

"All right, they are nice breasts. But you can put them away now."

Olivia got that look in her eyes and whipped off her own shirt, undid her bra, and set it flying across the room. It hooked itself on the handle of the extruder.

"Now it looks like the women's locker room. How fitting," Olivia said.

Maggie looked alarmed. "Remember group rules. No peer pressure."

"Oh, no. No pressure. Simply a choice. Either you take it off or we do. This is now the goddess clay dance, and appropriate attire is mandatory," Olivia replied.

Maggie looked at her two half-naked cohorts. "All right." She pulled off her shirt and removed her sports bra, flinging it out into the center of the room.

"It feels better, I admit. But if we're truly doing the dance, then we better do it right," Maggie said, picking up a handful of brown goo, smearing it across and around her chest. Then she took two fingers and made the sign of a widening gyre in the middle of her forehead.

"C'mon. I did your thing, and you can certainly do mine."

Olivia laughed. "My, you have blossomed."

She picked up a large scoop of clay and dumped it down her front, smearing her rather voluptuous breasts. Anna did the same and then stepped out to the small refrigerator and got three cold beers.

"Happy trails," she said.

They smiled and toasted one another. They began tromping methodically.

"I have to admit, the job has improved greatly. Not nearly so grueling," Olivia said.

Maggie took a drink. "Yes. Much improved."

The screen door opened, and Celia walked in, followed closely by another. Olivia and Anna looked up and smiled their welcome. Maggie turned crimson.

"She just arrived by taxi, " Celia said, looking at the clay-covered, half-naked women.

"Amanda, what are you doing here?"

"I should ask you the same question, only I think I'd rather not know the answer. I came to see what keeps you here and why you won't come home."

"It's not like I disappeared. You know where I am. I'm coming back, and then I'll straighten things out. But not until I'm good and ready."

"How much time do you need? Christ, you've had the whole damn summer."

Maggie felt her anger rising. "And I'll take the whole damn rest of my life if I so desire. You're a big girl now. You certainly don't need me around. What do you want me to do? Sit around that stupid old house and wait for you to have a crisis so I can be there for you? I have a right to a life of my own."

"That stupid old house is our home. Your home. What about your family? What are we supposed to do?"

"The same."

"So this is what hanging out in the desert does for you. It obviously boiled your brain. Great! A houseful of lunatics."

"I resent that," Olivia replied, scooping up more clay and rubbing it into her short hair and making it stand straight on end.

"Me, too," Anna chimed in.

Maggie looked at them and smiled. She looked at Celia, who shrugged her shoulders in helplessness. Maggie started to laugh, and the others joined in. Amanda stormed out of the studio, letting the screen door slam behind her.

"Does she remind you of anyone we all know?" Maggie said.

"Well, now that you mention it . . ." Olivia replied.

"I tell you, get rid of one uptight nazi queen and another takes her place. Nazi here, nazi there," Anna said. They all burst out laughing. Celia was amazed that Maggie was taking the whole episode so lightheartedly.

"Aren't you going to do anything about Amanda?" Celia asked.

"Have you got any suggestions?" Maggie asked.

"You should probably talk to her."

"And say what?' I refuse to tell her what she wants to hear."

"She's just confused about why you aren't coming home."

"No, she's selfish. She thinks that by coming here she can make me pack up and go back home, that puppy-dog eyes and temper tantrums will make mommy behave like she wants her to. I'm not going to play that game. If she's pissed off, so be it."

"Still, you two need to talk."

"No, we don't. I'm going back to settle my affairs when I damn well please and not a moment before."

"Maggie, come on. Be reasonable."

"No, Celia, you don't understand. I've spent my entire life putting my ambitions and desires behind everyone else's. I'm through. I already gave. Now it's my turn, and the sooner Amanda understands that the better."

Celia looked at her and nodded. "Okay."

Celia found Amanda sitting on the porch looking lost and forlorn.

"Do you need someone to talk to?" Celia asked.

"Yes, my mother, but she doesn't want to."

"I might prove a better substitute."

"I'm sorry. I don't mean to be rude, Celia. I just don't understand why she is here and doesn't want to come home. She won't explain anything to me, and it hurts. I feel like I've lost my whole family, both my parents. Dad dies, and Mom runs off. What am I supposed to think? Doesn't she care about me?"

"She cares, Amanda. I think this is just her way of dealing with your father's death. Maybe she needed some space. She is staying here as part of a team of women who help me in the studio during the summer. It keeps her busy, and she's made some new friends. Give her some time, Amanda. She's not running away. She is just getting to know herself again as a single woman, and that takes a lot of effort. Try to be patient."

"I know Dad's death has been hard on her, and I'm worried about her. She seems so different now. I don't think she wants to come back. Tell me honestly, Celia. Is she going to stay here?"

"Amanda, I'm not sure what she is planning to do. You two really need to talk. She'll come around. In the meantime, let's get your bags in the house. You can have a shower and a cool drink, and you'll feel much better."

"Thanks, Celia. For everything."


"Where is she?" Maggie asked as Celia handed her a towel. Maggie showered in the outdoor stall that Celia had devised. The cubicle was walled by lattice and covered in thirsty desert vines.

"She's getting cleaned up. Maggie, she's pretty upset. Be tender."

"It doesn't matter how I say it, Celia. She's not going to like what it means. I am not going back. I am going to live here and make pottery, and I don't care who likes it or doesn't."

Celia shook her head. "This is not going to be pretty."

"No, it's not. So hang on to your hat because here I go."


Amanda combed her hair in front of the mirror. She had her mother's thick, curly hair and she hated it because it wouldn't do what she wanted. She saw her mother's reflection in the mirror as she stood in the door frame.

"Can we talk?" Maggie asked.

"That's what I've been trying to do," Amanda replied, setting the brush down and turning around to face her mother.

As Maggie sat on the bed she felt an odd sensation of calmness. She knew she was doing what she had to in order to make her life what she so desperately wanted — hers.

"You're not going back, are you?"

At least her daughter wasn't stupid. But she took the bang out of Maggie's intended rabbit-punch approach.

"No, I'm not going back."

"Why not?"

"Because there is nothing there for me anymore."

"And you like it here better, I suppose."

"Yes, I like it here better."

"But what about me? About how I feel about all this, this sudden change of heart."

"I wouldn't call it sudden," Maggie replied. She

thought, I've spent my whole life waiting for this moment, the moment when I could say good-bye to a life of compromise.

"How can you say that? You leave me a message on the machine, rush off to Phoenix, and stay away the whole of spring and summer after you said you were only staying a week. And now you're never coming back, and you don't call that sudden? No, maybe you're right. It's not sudden, it's crazy. You're acting crazy. Grown women do not run off and leave everything behind."

"But desperate women do."

"Now you're desperate?"

"No, not exactly. I simply am making some much needed changes in my life."

"Which means excluding me."

"I'm not excluding you from anything."

"You think that you can just relinquish all your ties with a swish of your hand and owe nothing, that you can just pretend nothing before existed."

"What could I possibly owe? I've paid my dues. What do you want me to do? Spend the rest of my life creating a shrine for your father? He had his days of glory. What could I possibly owe you? I raised you. I loved you, and now you're grown. Why do you need me?"

"You're my mother."

"I can still be your mother and not live two doors down. I'm not abandoning you. I'm taking hold of my own life. You shouldn't begrudge me that, Amanda. I gave you twenty-six years of my life. I'm entitled to the rest."

Amanda sat on the bed next to her mother. Their identical eyes met.

"Do you regret those years?"

"Only when you're being a pain-in-the-ass."

"What!"

"I'm kidding, Amanda. No, I don't regret any of them, except maybe when you were thirteen. You were really a pain-in-the-ass then. You have improved. I love you. I'm not leaving. I'm just relocating."

"What about the house?" Amanda asked.

Maggie looked down at her hands. This would be the truly hard part, and it was going to hurt. Amanda *loved* that house. Maggie would give it to her, but she couldn't afford to do that. It would have to be sold.

"I'm going to sell it."

"You can't!" Amanda said, standing up.

"I have to, Amanda."

"It's all we have left of him."

"He was more than the house and the things in it. You have your feelings for him, your memories."

"But it was our house. I grew up there. You can't sell it."

"It needs other people, another family to grow up in it. It's too big for one person."

"How can you even think of someone else living there? It's our house. How can you want to get rid of it?"

"Amanda, I don't need it anymore. It's time to move on."

"You don't need it, you don't need me. I think you're sorry you ever married Dad or had me. We were nothing to you. Well, you don't mean anything to me either," Amanda said, running from the room.

Celia was on the couch reading. She saw Amanda

run down the stairs with tears streaming down her face.

Maggie followed her. "Amanda, wait."

She looked at Celia.

"That went well, don't you think?"

"Come sit and have some tea."

"I think I need something a little stronger." Maggie sat next to Celia and took a long drink of her beer.

"She thinks I'm deserting the family and Harold's memory. I can't live there. I won't live there. I never should have lived there."

"What do mean you never should have lived there?"

"I married Harold because I couldn't have you. He was the next best thing. He reminded me of you. You might as well know that I loved you. I've always loved you."

"Oh, Maggie," Celia said, holding out her arms. "I'm so sorry. I never knew. I didn't think it was possible. I didn't want you to get hurt."

"I won't go back."

"No, you won't. Not ever," Celia said, nestling her face in her lover's neck.


Amanda watched from the window as the others packed up. A multicolored collection of backpacks were stuffed into the bed of the truck. They were heading for the canyon lands of southern Utah.

Amanda could not be enticed to go. She was still

angry and hurt. She barely spoke to her mother, yet she didn't leave. No one pressed her. They left her sitting cross-legged in front of the television, apparently engrossed in a program. She muttered good-bye. She listened to the truck as it pulled away, and the ping and tick of Olivia's bright orange Volkswagen bus.

They headed for the Anasazi Indian ruins in the canyons of Grand Gulch. It was a trip Celia took at the end of every summer, never growing tired of the canyons and the ruins. The trip sealed the end of the season with a sense of spiritual renewal that she could get only by sitting in a kiva or a storage room built of earth and straw.

The caravan arrived early the next morning. They had coffee and watched the sunrise across the expanse of southern desert. Gnarled juniper trees dotted the orange landscape. Each woman grabbed her pack, and Celia led them to the widening labyrinth of the canyon.


Maggie thought about Amanda. Her daughter was right in accusing her of regretting her life with Harold. She had sold herself short, and now she knew it.

"It taught you to appreciate this life, didn't it?" Olivia had said on the drive to the canyons. "You don't have to have totally abstained from men in order to be a lesbian. Lots of women find out later."

Maggie looked over at her friend.

"I wish I had your confidence in the idea that things happen for a reason. I feel like it was all a waste. That makes me sad; I squandered something precious."

"I'm sure there were moments when you felt happy, or had some sense of being complete."

Maggie looked out the window at the black countryside as it whizzed by.

"No, Olivia, it was more like this drive. Tunnel vision through a dark landscape, but with no apparent aim in mind. Unhappy, but not knowing why. I just staggered through."

"So feeling good about your life now, feeling full, makes the emptiness more acute?"

"Exactly."

"My only advice to you would be, Chalk it up to experience. Don't let the past fuck up what you've got going now. You served your time, now move on."

"Oh, Liv, if only it was that easy."

"Maggie, you can make it easy."

She had tried, but the past hung like a low-lying cloud. She no longer wanted or needed to go back to the house, to Amanda, to her mother, to all those responsibilities. Dread was creeping up on her. The dread of being away from Celia, of sleeping in that bed alone again, of going to the cemetery, of having dinner at her mother's, of trying to explain what she was going through to people who wouldn't understand.

She pulled her pack higher on her shoulders, set her sights on the next curve in the canyon, and vowed to ignore those thoughts until she had to face them. I will get through this, and I'll come back. I'll stand on that porch and know I'm home, finally home.


Setting up camp never felt so welcome. A seven-mile hike through the winding, sandy canyon floor carrying a heavy backpack was no easy task, and each woman took her pack off with relief.

"Well, for an old gal you sure can hike," Olivia said to Celia.

Celia smiled. "This is our usual spot. It's close to the stream, and there are three ruins not far from here that we can explore either tonight or in the morning. Everybody find a spot for your tent, and let's get comfortable."

Maggie helped Celia put up their tent. Water was located, dinner started, and soon the bottle of tequila was making its way around the small campfire.

Maggie took a swig from the bottle and shoved the lemon into her mouth quickly. She winced, and Olivia laughed.

"You're so butch now," Olivia said.

"Am not."

"Are too."

"Am I?" Maggie asked, suddenly thinking about going back to the Midwest and about her reception there.

"Do I look like a lesbian?"

"I don't know. What do lesbians look like?" Olivia asked.

"They come in different sizes, a variety of shapes, different colors, some dress like boys, some like girls, and some don't dress at all," Anna replied, smiling.

"Very funny. What I mean is, things like short hair and no makeup. Are they going to know by looking?" Maggie asked anxiously.

"You look the same to me. You look like Maggie," Olivia replied.

Maggie wasn't convinced. Amanda had commented on her appearance. She acted like Maggie was committing some atrocity, as if she wasn't upholding her end of the feminine bargain. Amanda attributed it to peer pressure, happily assuring her mother things would change. She would feel different when she got back home. Maggie just smiled, wondering if Amanda had picked up on the fact she was surrounded by lesbians. It probably hadn't crossed her mind. Not yet at least.

Maggie was lost in thought until Celia touched her hand. She looked up at Celia. They smiled, knowing that what they had was right.

"I've been thinking. Maybe I'd like to get a tattoo," Maggie said.

"Why?" Celia asked.

"It's the lesbian thing to do," Maggie replied.

"Are you afraid you'll go back and forget you are one?"

"With you to remind me, never," Maggie said, squeezing Celia's arm.

"Oh, how sweet," Olivia said facetiously.

"What kind of a tattoo?" Celia asked.

"I want the Kokopelli right here on my ankle, the flute player, the trickster playing in the desert. It will be a reminder of all the things I want to be."

Celia looked at the seriousness clouding Maggie's face. She hadn't thought that going back would be so hard for Maggie. She felt a pang of guilt for being insensitive.

"I'm sorry. I hadn't realized how difficult going back is going to be for you, that you are worried."

"It's not the going back so much as saying I'm packing up permanently to live somewhere else. Amanda is not going to make things easy, and who knows what she's figured out? She is not one to keep quiet."

"Maybe you should visit my mother," Celia said, laughing.

"That would go over big. I'm sure there has already been talk. Can you imagine how well it will go over when everyone figures out that we're lovers?"

"Another tried and true lesbian corrupts a perfectly good heterosexual," Olivia said.

Kate and Madeline laughed until they began to roll about the sand with tears streaming down their faces.

"I don't find it that amusing. That's exactly how everyone is going to see it."

"Didn't you?" Olivia asked slyly.

"No, I did not," Celia replied, her feathers more than a little ruffled.

"I guess we know who seduced who then, don't we?" Olivia said, taking another drink of tequila and passing it to Maggie.

"I would have grown old waiting. Somebody had to do something to get the ball rolling," Maggie said, smiling at Celia.

"I still don't understand what's so funny," Celia said.

"That straight people always think it's the dyke who does the seducing. It's usually not, but straight people always think so. They've got it all wrong. That's what is so funny," Madeline said.

"That may be true, but it doesn't help my image. I'm still going to look like the one who corrupted Maggie," Celia said. She was suddenly beginning to appreciate the gravity of Maggie's situation. "This is going to be ugly."

"You really think so? It is the nineties, you know. People change," Olivia said.

"You haven't met our mothers," Celia said. "My mother thinks I'm some sort of oversexed seductress. She'll talk Josephine into believing I poisoned Maggie."

"I'll try to set them straight, no pun intended, but you're probably right. You're going to look like the bad guy, regardless," Maggie told her.

"Are you really serious about this tattoo? If you are, I could find a petroglyph that had definite significance to remind me of this summer and the things that were special about it," Olivia said.

"She's getting sentimental, you guys. This is a rare moment," Anna said, giving Olivia a gentle shove.

"I can be sensitive. I've had a really good summer, and I've really enjoyed the time I spent with all of you. It was special, and I'll always remember it."

"Ditto," Kate said.

"And I think we should each get one. Group tattoo time," Madeline said.

"Well, I'd hate to miss out on this orgy of prickly pain. I'm in," Anna said.

Maggie looked at Celia.

"If I remember correctly, group rules cite there will be no peer pressure," Celia said.

"No, there's no pressure. But if you're scared, we understand," Olivia chided.

"C'mon now, the idea is not to coerce anyone. It'll ruin the moment, and the tattoo won't have honest karma," Maggie said.

"Tattoos with karma. Oh, Maggie, you are going to give them a scare when you get home. And just for the record, I am not afraid. It's just that tattoos are so permanent. It's not like fashion or hairdos. You can't make the damn things go away."

"That's the idea. A tattoo will forever remind you of a point in your life when something really good happened," Olivia said.

"Are you guys counting two sappy moments?" Anna said.

"Or something good coupled with a radical change," Maggie said.

"Let me get this straight. You want a tattoo to commemorate your switching sides of the fence," Celia said.

"It is a pivotal point in one's life," Kate said.

"It's like the poem you wrote after you got your first tattoo, 'Tattoo My Esprit from the Conformity of Mind,' " Madeline said to Kate.

"Exactly, and it seems Maggie is feeling some of those same vibes," Kate said.

"You know, for such a young bunch you all are pretty much in tune," Celia said as she began to reevaluate her position. "Not that age inspires wisdom." She looked at Maggie. "Maybe you're right. We all need little reminders of where we have been and where we are going. Do you remember that part in *Moby Dick* when Melville talks about the skin being a text and the importance of marking it?" Celia asked Maggie.

"I do. That was one of my favorite parts."

"Does this mean you'll do it?" Olivia asked.

"Yes, and I know exactly which petroglyph I'm choosing."

"Share. Which one?" Anna asked.

"It's the one with two Kokopellis, the one I call narcissistic copulation," Celia replied.

"Why that one?" Olivia asked.

"You can't be serious," Maggie said, hoping this choice was in jest, a payback of sorts.

"I am serious. The way I see it, the two figures are identical. They are not distinguishable by sex or definite signs of gender. Those primitive people had a different view of sexuality. It could be one of the first homosexual symbols, for all we know. And since I've spent most of my adult life being a lesbian and engaging in what the dominant culture oftentimes views as narcissistic copulation, that symbol becomes the physical manifestation of my text."

"For someone who wasn't even considering the possibility of getting a tattoo you certainly have thoroughly analyzed your choice and its meaning," Olivia said eyeing Celia curiously.

"I just never had a good enough reason, a strong enough love of duality, to want to adorn my body with a symbol so permanent, that's all."

"And now you're saying you do?" Maggie asked.

"Yes, my darling, now I do."

"Pass me the tequila and stop being so sappy," Olivia said.

"Boy, the sentimental stint certainly didn't last long," Celia replied, handing her the bottle.

"Olivia, that's not nice. Finding your other half is absolutely beautiful, an event to be cherished, one that is not easily achieved," Kate said.

"Nor easily kept," Anna said, ruefully.

"What's that supposed to mean?" Olivia asked.

"I think you know already," Anna replied.

"Are you referring to our failed love affair?" Olivia asked.

"You two were lovers?" Maggie asked, shocked by the revelation.

"Yes, it's the beautiful rise and demise of our ongoing relationship. We just can't seem to get away from each other," Anna said, shrugging her shoulders.

"Yes, we just go through periods of dating other people," Olivia said.

"And of missing the one person you really enjoy the most," Anna said.

"You miss me? Really?" Olivia said.

"No, I just follow you around for no apparent reason," Anna said.

"What's the problem?" Madeline asked.

"If we knew that, we wouldn't be having this discussion, now would we? We'd be part of the love-twins cult, living happily ever after basking in the warm glow of each other's undying love and adoration," Olivia said.

"Now I would call that an obvious expression of frustration," Celia said.

"Listen, you love birds. Do you think I like existing in this state of limbo? Yes, I love Anna. But when we act like lovers we fall apart; when we act like friends we go on forever. If I could stop, change it, make it go away, or get it really going, don't you think I would? Do you think I like not having someone to share my life with? That it's pleasant or something? That always worrying Anna will someday find someone and walk out of my life forever is what I want?" Olivia said, taking a swig of the bottle out of turn.

Anna looked at her, puzzled. "Are you serious?"

"No, I made it all up for the hell of it."

"Oh," Anna said. "May I have a drink of that?"


Madeline and Kate wandered off to explore the kiva after breakfast. It made Maggie think about what Olivia had said about the love-twins cult. When Celia had told Maggie that Madeline and Kate were coming, she said they were lovers. After they had been at the ranch a while, Celia was convinced they were mystical twin lovers that traveled through time, losing each other only to find one another again and again, perfecting their lives and their love with each pass through the realm of life.

At first Maggie laughed at what she thought was Celia's preposterous idea, but the more time she spent with them the more she began to see what Celia did. They were mystical love twins. How else could two such people find each other and become such perfect complements?

Maggie watched them scale the small incline that led to the kiva, helping each other along, holding hands, playing. Will we be like that? Maggie wondered.

Celia came up behind and kissed her neck. "I missed you."

"But I haven't gone anywhere."

"I can still miss you," Celia replied.

"Whatever are you going to do when I'm gone?"

"Miss you ever so much. Can't I come with you?"

"No, we decided already. You have too much going on here right now, and Minneapolis is not going to be a vacation. And I would prefer to leave you out of the familial invectives."

"Are you sure you don't have ulterior motives?"

"Such as?" Maggie replied, shaking the water off the breakfast dishes.

"Such as in keeping me from reliving certain unpleasant memories."

"Do you really think I'm that astute and sensitive?"

"Yes," Celia said, taking her in her arms.

"Well, you're only half right. I don't want you to go through another disownment on my account. I remember how mean people were to you."

"What is the other half of your reasoning?"

"I need to process this alone. I don't want you to think that I'm cutting you off, but I don't want you to see my old life. I don't want you to have that memory of me."

"I understand."

"And are you relieved?"

Celia smiled. "Very relieved. I would go if you really wanted me to, but I'm glad you don't."

# Chapter Seven

Maggie sat on a rock shelf meditating while the others explored a nearby ruin. It was so quiet in the canyon that she could think without distraction and let her mind flow where it wanted. She was dreaming. The idea came out of nothingness. She indulged it. She was no longer afraid of her dreams. She no longer hid from them.

Later when she lay in Celia's arms listening to the buzz and click of nocturnal creatures, she worked through her dream, gave it substance, grasped its content.

"Celia?"

"Yes, darling."

"I have an idea."

"Should I be afraid to ask?"

"No, I don't think so."

"You aren't going to color your hair purple?"

"No, Amanda beat me to that one. It's hard to imagine her so stodgy now. She is the same age as Olivia and Anna, yet she is already so set in her ways."

"Perhaps you can help her regain the joy she lost somewhere."

"No, she'll have to do that on her own. She needs her own set of keys for that."

"Yes, I think you're right. What's your idea?"

"I want to turn the ranch into a women's art center. Keep the apprentices on, pay them a salary, make lots of pottery, teach classes, turn it into a community. There's land enough, labor enough, enough of everything to make it work. We need to share what we've created this summer with many others."

"Maggie, it's a nice idea, but it's not feasible. We would be way out of our league. You're talking lots of time, money, and planning."

"We have all that. You've made it work on a small scale; it could also work on a much larger scale."

"It takes money, Maggie. I don't have it."

"But I do. I have more than I knew what to do with until today. Today I know. I know it would work. It's been waiting to work. You've already laid the groundwork. All you need is a major investor. Now you have one."

"Maggie, you're dreaming."

"It's not a dream you haven't had. You can't say you haven't thought of it. You don't want to let the apprentices go. You've had to let too many of them go. Create a place where their talents can really be used. I know you don't like sending them back into a world that crushes them. I know you've felt that weight at the end of every summer. What if you could employ the ones who want to stay?"

"You're not being practical."

"I've been practical and safe all my life. It's only since I threw caution to the wind that I've begun to live. Don't limit yourself, Celia. Take the risk. Think of it: an art center, a commune, a business, a school, a place to live, a movement. My God, we'll have to come up with a logo."

Celia rolled over and groaned. "You're out of control, Maggie. Stop!"

"I can't. I can't stop thinking about it. I want to do this, Celia. Promise me you'll think about it."

Celia rolled over to face her, leaning up on one elbow. She could see the fire in her lover's eyes. "I promise to think about." How could she refuse? It wasn't as if she hadn't dreamed of it herself. But it was always a dream, a frightening dream. She was not an entrepreneur. She needed someone else's spark.

Maggie kissed her. "Thank you. Just let your mind soar with it. Imagine. Promise?"

"Promise."

Maggie kissed her again. She felt desire, and reached gently for Celia.

\* \* \* \* \*

Olivia and Anna sat on the rock that bordered the stream soaking their feet. The cold water felt good as it ran across their feet and made rivulets in the smooth water.

"It's almost over, and you know how I hate endings."

"We could always come back next summer," Anna replied.

Olivia looked at her. "You know as well as I do that too many things can happen in a year's time to even think of a plan like that. When it's over, it's over. I wish we could stay. That's what I really want. I want to hang out in the desert and make pots. To hell with rest of the world. I just want a little corner to work in."

"You want a sanctuary."

"A sanctuary where living could have some dignity, a sanctuary from all the insanity."

Anna took her friend's hand and kissed it. "I'd be willing to try. Maybe we could find a place and try being together again." She took Olivia's face in her hands and kissed the tears away.


It was at the bar in Flagstaff with all of them sitting at a glossy, well-worn, thick oak table that Maggie revealed her plan, one that Celia had tentatively agreed to. Maggie's excitement had been contagious. Celia liked her life being so full, and she wasn't eager to see it emptied again.

They sat in a circle around the table, sunburned and dusty, each with a glossy bandage covering her tattoo. They were drinking pitchers of beer to take the edge off their painful experience.

Maggie explained her plan and waited for their reaction. Smiles crept across all their faces, except for Olivia's. She burst into tears and turned for Anna's arms.

"What's wrong?" Maggie asked.

"Nothing. Absolutely nothing. It's beautiful, perfect. We wanted this so bad and now it's happening. They're happy tears, believe me," Anna told her.

Olivia nodded her agreement.

"You guys really want to stay? See if we can make this work?" Celia asked, still dazed that the ranch meant as much to other women as it did to herself.

"We didn't want to leave, but summer was over and so was the program," Madeline replied.

"I have never felt as at peace as I do at the ranch. It's the place I was looking for and couldn't find," Kate said.

"Can we farm?" Anna asked, looking earnestly at Celia.

"Farm?" asked Celia.

"Yeah, like grow all of our own stuff and some to sell too. Think about it. Food is a major expense."

"Brew our own beer?" Olivia said, smacking her lips.

"It's worth a try. This could work," Anna said emphatically.

Celia smiled and took Maggie's hand. "You were right."

When they returned to the ranch, it was with anticipation and not the dread of packing up shortly.

It was night when they pulled up in front of the house.

Amanda was gone.

"I thought she might be," said Maggie, setting the note down on the kitchen table and picking up the plane ticket. Maggie looked at the date on the ticket. Amanda had generously given her a week's notice.

"You and Amanda do have one thing in common — plane tickets."

"Yes, but look how well the first one turned out," Celia replied.

"Will I be so fortunate again?"

"Yes, because the next one will be the one back."

"You noticed it's not a round-trip ticket. She is in for a surprise."

"Does she think if she wills something it will simply happen because she wants it to?" Anna asked, suddenly angry at the young woman she hardly knew.

"What a wretched little bitch," said Olivia.

"Olivia! That's not nice. She's Maggie's child," Kate reprimanded.

"No, she's right. Amanda is a wretched little bitch. I just wish I knew why. What did I do? What could I have done to make her less hostile? She has no room for the beautiful things in life. She never has."

"That's too bad. You'd be a neat mom to have. I wish you could have been mine," Olivia replied.

Maggie turned to look at her. "Thank you."

\* \* \* \* \*

Walking out to their cottage, Anna took Olivia's hand.

"You know, you're starting to lose some of your rough edges."

"What do you mean?" Olivia asked.

"What you said to Maggie. That was nice, and I know you meant it."

"And do you like these softer edges?"

"Yes, very much."

"I'm glad."

Celia found Maggie in the bathtub. She sat on the bench near the edge of the tub, took the sponge, and gently washed Maggie's back, thinking how much she would miss her, her touch, her laugh, her hands, her lips.

"Are you going?"

"Yes, I suppose I should. Will you miss me?"

"No, not at all."

"You beast," said Maggie, reaching for her.

Celia melted into her touch. "More than I could ever tell you."

"Please, don't cry. We can't have two of us blubbering."

"I know. Just be careful. No jaywalking, no answering doors to strangers, no fast car rides."

"Why? Are you afraid I won't come back?"

"I let you go once. I couldn't bear to do it twice."

"I'm coming back."

"Promise?"

"Promise."

* * * * *

"She better come back," said Olivia as the four of them watched Maggie leave.

"She will. She loves Celia. She loves this place. And she loves us. She'll be back," Anna said, putting her arm around Olivia's shoulders.

Maggie wouldn't let them go with her to the airport. She told them that when she had come from Minneapolis she had taken a cab to the airport. She couldn't bear good-byes in such sterile public environments. She'd rather have a nice dinner with them and then leave. And they had had a nice dinner.

They had taken their bandages off their tattoos after dinner and hugged one another other goodnight. But now it was morning and she was leaving. They all felt it acutely. Each day was going to seem long while she was away.

"We'll have a big party when she gets back, have Karen and those guys come down. We'll make a weekend of it. C'mon, this is going to be hard enough without all these long faces," Celia told them.

The dust died down on the road and, except for Olivia, they left the porch one by one.

"Take care pretty lady. Don't let them hurt you too bad," said Olivia to the now empty horizon. Maybe that was why it was so hard to let her go. They all knew the difficulty of informing the straight people in your life of your new love. It takes more than persuasion; it takes courage. Olivia said a silent prayer and walked off into the early morning.

# Chapter Eight

As the wheels of the plane hit the ground, Maggie was jolted from her daydream. She was remembering the rainstorm, the electricity in the air, the brilliant burning sunset, the black sky, the green clawlike fronds of thrashing palms as the wind caught them, the last night she lay in Celia's arms. They had made love during the storm, and when the rain stopped the air had smelled so clean.

Maggie sat patiently while the other travelers scrambled for their overhead luggage. She was second to last getting off the plane. She felt no hurry.

Instead, she pictured her soul stretching long across the miles between Phoenix and St. Paul. She knew her mother and her daughter sat anxiously waiting and watching each woman's face as she came off the plane, wondering when hers would appear.

Maggie felt instantly claustrophobic, closed in by her family, escorted home like a truant schoolgirl soon to be persuaded of the futility of her wild ways. Generations of mediocrity, Maggie thought. Like mother, like daughter, except this daughter was breaking away. Amanda would marry out of a sense of duty and fear. Maggie had been there. She had left passion to others. But no longer. Would they read it in her face? Feel it in her touch? Only the days would tell.

When she spotted Maggie, Amanda beamed with her success. Her mother breathed a sigh of relief. Maggie kissed them both, took their hands, and followed them to the baggage carousel, politely and accurately responding to their questions. Yes, the flight was fine. Everything was fine, for this evening. But Maggie could see it in their eyes. Amanda had been telling stories.

She pictured them having lunch and discussing the proposed mental state of the truant. They knew where they stood, decided upon a plan of attack, and joined forces against this unknown enemy. Were they measuring her now? Deciding when to probe, when to seduce, when to engage in battle?

Maggie steeled herself against the onslaught. She was outnumbered, perhaps would be outmaneuvered, but she had her own agenda. They could not interfere with a widow's desire to sell a house, liquidate assets, and move to the southwest. Everyone got her share, and Harold had been explicit with the details. Their only hope was coercion, but Maggie knew that love, passion, and drive are more powerful than contrived guilt. She felt strong. It was all decided long before her daughter's and mother's lunches, dinners, teas, and plots.

The city lights whirled and blurred as the white Lincoln sedan sped across the Mississippi River. Skyscrapers were sprinkled with lights. She had made the drive from the airport to Minneapolis more times than she could remember, driving Harold back from some medical conference in a far-off city.

The sky was heavy with impending rain. Maggie felt it coming, and with it a stuffy depression. She hated the dreary rain in the Midwest.

She didn't want to be sad in front of Amanda and her mother. They would think she was weakening, that the stress of going away and now coming back was too much for her. She would never give them that satisfaction. She couldn't afford to, so she swallowed her silent, wracking sob.

"Come for dinner tomorrow night. We'll talk," her mother said.

Maggie suppressed the urge to ask, Talk about what? Instead, she smiled her response, nodding her head.

"Do you want me to stay?" Amanda asked.

"No, I think buying the plane ticket was enough. I'm fine. I'll call you tomorrow."

Amanda looked at her, puzzled and uncertain of Maggie's intent.

"All right."

After they left, Maggie made herself a pot of tea.

Staring into her cupboards she suddenly hated her crockery. It was so plain, neat, refined, and without character. She wondered at the woman who purchased it. The whole house seemed foreign. Maybe Olivia was right about having more than one life in a lifetime.

She slung her suitcase on the bed and began to unpack, making little shrines of the rocks, sticks, and pottery she had brought back. Shrines to remind, shrines to worship, shrines to keep her focused. She found a box in the garage and neatly stacked her old dishes away and replaced them with ones she and Celia had made.

She took photographs from the summer and taped them to the front of the fridge. She rolled up the Oriental rug that had graced the living room floor for years and replaced it with a Navajo rug that Celia had bought her. Tomorrow she would go to the garden center and buy some cacti. She would get through this, and she would go back.

She wandered around the house like a guest. Her furniture was all well-made, upper-middle class, eastern. Dark mahogany, brocade floral prints, drapes with sheers, heavy Oriental rugs, tasteful knick-knacks, and appropriate prints all breathed safe, suburban attitudes. No, her possessions wouldn't be hard to part with. They weren't her; they never had been.

The sheets were clean and cold. She hated sleeping alone. Children and women without lovers slept alone. Rain beat against the window and Maggie pulled the comforter up around her neck. She was cold and scared. What was Celia doing now? Was she awake, looking at the ceiling, thinking of her, feeling lost and alone? Or was she glad for the space, relieved not to have to think of another?

She had been relieved sometimes when Harold was gone. She enjoyed being alone to wander, to read, to nap, to not think about what to have for dinner. It was like being recreationally single, only you didn't have to worry about not having someone. Your someone would come home eventually.

She had felt guilty for not missing him as she should, for the little pitch she felt when he was back and she had to start thinking in two's again when one was so much simpler. Did Celia feel the same way? Maggie didn't.

She was drowning in love. She prayed that their love wouldn't end, that both of them could make it work, and that all the things they hadn't found in others could be found in each other.

She got out of bed and walked to the window, staring out into the blackness. Love is wondrous and dangerous. Her summer had been so full. The fall would be so empty. How quickly could she get out of here and back to Celia? She knew the answer: Not quickly enough. She jumped when the phone rang.

"Hello," said Maggie, trying to keep the inquisitiveness out of her voice.

"What's wrong?" Celia asked.

"Nothing. How are you? God, I miss you already."

"I couldn't sleep. I didn't wake you, did I?"

"No, I'm busy wandering around the house, plotting my escape, and missing you. I love you."

"I love you, too. Try to get some sleep, though, otherwise you'll end up comatose."

"And then I'll be easier prey for the vultures."

"Exactly. Speaking of vultures, how are they?"

"Full of strategies, I can feel it, the hair-on-the-back-of-your-neck stuff. But I'm all right. I am going to get through this."

"I know you are."

Maggie was sitting at the kitchen table drinking coffee, reading. The doorbell jarred her concentration. She got up, puzzled. She wasn't expecting anyone. She cautiously opened the door to a delivery man who held a box and asked her to sign.

The box contained a dozen yellow roses. The card read, "No new girlfriend. Eagerly awaiting your arrival. Love, Celia." Maggie smiled, remembering having chided Celia about finding another girlfriend in her absence. She knew it was absurd at the time, but she needed reassurance and Celia had given it.

Smiling, she put the roses in a vase on the kitchen table and stuck the card in the center of the burst of yellow. Love with a sense of humor. Maggie liked that.

Her relationship with Harold could best be described as somber. Being back in the house made her keenly aware of the differences. She would take tears and laughter any day over silence and pursed lips. She was grateful she had the opportunity to experience the difference.

Later in the day, Amanda found her going through Harold's desk. Maggie hadn't realized how intact she had left everything. It was as if Harold could walk through that door at any moment. She was relieved he couldn't. It would have broken his heart to know that the two women he loved most loved each other. It probably would have killed him. Being left for another woman almost had killed him. What would he have done if she hadn't been there? What would she have done if he hadn't needed her?

Harold and Maggie had both been amputees that managed to form some mismatched whole. If he hadn't died, she would not have her new life, her right life. She wondered how many other people wandered around living the wrong life, not consciously knowing but sensing that some crucial ingredient was missing, and didn't know where to look.

"What are you doing?" Amanda asked.

"Sorting, thinking, trying to figure out what to do with this stuff," Maggie replied, waving her arm at the walls lined with medical books.

"Why not leave them where they are?" Amanda asked.

"What, and try to sell the house to a doctor?"

"You're still thinking of selling the house?"

"Does that surprise you? It was the reason I came back."

"I thought you were back to stay."

"Amanda, stop playing ignorant. You know as well as I do that I came back to clear up loose ends and that I'm going back. I made that abundantly clear when you visited, and I haven't changed my mind. Let's go have tea and talk about more pleasant things. You need to catch me up on your life."

Amanda allowed herself to be led into the kitchen where Maggie set about making tea. Amanda looked at the roses and picked up the card. Maggie's stomach took a quick turn.

Amanda read the card and frowned. "What's that supposed to mean?"

"It's fairly self-explanatory."

"What does she want with you?"

"My body, can't you see?" Maggie said, sashaying a hip forward, a hand behind her neck.

Amanda did not laugh. She looked perturbed. "Very funny. What is going on with you two?"

"Haven't you guessed by now?" Maggie knew she was dodging the question, but coming out was never easy. She'd heard the horror stories.

"No, I haven't done any guessing. I want you to tell me, for once, what is going on, what happened while you were down there. Why are you so different now?"

"Does it matter?"

"Yes, it matters. I have a right to know."

"And what right is that?" Maggie said, annoyed at being suddenly cornered and pressed.

"I am your daughter."

"That you are," Maggie replied, looking defiantly at her. I know what to say, I know what I am.

"You're sleeping with her, aren't you?" Amanda declared, her fear of the answer written in her eyes.

Maggie put her hand on the countertop, her thumb running back and forth across the hard edge.

"Yes, I'm sleeping with her. I love Celia, and I intend to spend the rest of my life with her."

"You know what that makes you, don't you?"

"Yes."

"Aren't you a little old to be taking this up?"

"I wasn't aware that sexuality had an age limit."

"I'll have to tell Gram."

"Tell whomever you'd like."

153

"You're not going to go about flaunting this, are you?"

"You seem to have no trouble deciding who to tell. I certainly have more of a prerogative than you. After all, it isn't your affair unless you make it so. Just once, Amanda, think about the consequences of your actions."

"That advice would be better spent on yourself," Amanda said. "After all, I'm not the one who turned into an irresponsible pervert after her husband died."


"She called you a what?" Celia asked, pressing the phone close and wishing it was Maggie's face and not just the tease of her voice.

"An irresponsible pervert. I miss you. I feel so disorganized and helpless. I don't know where to begin."

"I miss you, too. You'll get it together. Find an estate broker to sell the stuff and find a lesbian or gay realtor. Minneapolis is full of them."

"Why do I need a lesbian or gay realtor?"

"Support the family, the community, and all that. Besides, it saves a lot of strange or embarrassing questions. You'll be more comfortable."

"How do I find one?"

"We did send you off woefully unprepared, Maggie. You're a babe in the woods. Go to the women's bookstore by Loring Park. I can't remember the name of it. They'll have the paper with a listing of all community-sponsored businesses."

"I know where that store is. I used to drive by it when I dropped Amanda off at school."

"See, it'll work out."

"You're right."

"Now hurry up and get going. And get back here, dammit, before I have to come and get you."

"Would you?" Maggie teased.

"You know I would."

Maggie had never been in a lesbian bookstore. She'd driven past it the entire time Amanda had gone to community college. It was funny to live in a place your whole life and only know a few parts of it. Ironically, she'd gotten married around the corner at the Basilica.

Maggie parked the car and locked it. She felt scared but she stopped herself from setting the car alarm. Two young women sat drinking coffee at the café adjacent to the store. She suddenly felt conspicuous, driving an expensive, sleek BMW, easing it into the small parking space. It was a car with attitude, and it wasn't wasted on the women who watched her walk across the street.

She felt like the doctor's wife again, moneyed and protected. She'd sell the car and buy a Jeep or something sturdy. There was the Mercedes, too. God, there was a lot of property to be divested. House, cars, furniture. She had a life to trade in.

She tried to walk nonchalantly through the door. A string of brass bells sounded her arrival, and she straightened her shoulders to appear confident. She knew she was not convincing.

"New in town? Haven't seen you before. Welcome. Anything I can help you with?" asked a small woman with short, dark, spiky hair and a zillion earrings, including one in her nose.

Maggie smiled. She tried not to stare but yet

make eye contact at the same time. Celia was right. She was a babe in the woods. With her it was easy to be confident and secure. Alone here, it was different.

"I was looking for one of the lesbian and gay newspapers."

"They don't come out again until Thursday. We're all out at the moment. I'll hold one back for you when they come out if you like. Sometimes they go fast, especially in this neighborhood. Center of the community, I call it. What's your name?"

"Maggie. Maggie Lawrence."

"All right, Maggie, consider it done. Anything else you're interested in? We've got a bit of everything."

"I could use some fiction," Maggie said, looking around and thinking that the bookshelves at home had become slim pickings.

"Highbrow or trash?"

"More on the literary side, but not dry. A good story."

"Okay follow me."

Maggie watched her stroll from behind the counter. She wore long black underwear underneath cutoff jeans and a gold tight-fitting leotard top. She must be all of twenty-five. Maggie found herself admiring her backside. It felt strange sometimes to appreciate women's bodies, their curves and angles, their soft skin, their gentle touch.

The young woman smiled coyly when she caught Maggie scoping her out. She didn't seem to mind. Instead, she looked interested. I'm old enough to be your mother. Of course, that never deterred Libby. But I am an attached woman, Maggie thought, smiling in a proud, secure way.

They went through the books and Maggie selected some two dozen, plus she had made a new friend, Sam. Picking out books had led to several conversations, and the two were going out for coffee when Maggie returned on Thursday to pick up her paper.

Walking out of the store, Maggie wasn't sure how she had come by the coffee engagement. Sam had decided that since Maggie was new to the community she needed a tour guide. There was something about being "family," as everyone called it, that pulled people together. Whatever it was, it was good.

Having gotten over that hurdle, she prepared herself for the next one, which was dinner with her mother and daughter. Maggie was certain Amanda had spilled her findings in horror to Gram Josephine. The two had always been close. Maggie had never been close to either of them.

She had done all the things mothers were supposed to do, but Amanda had probably sensed that Maggie's heart wasn't in it. Children seem to have a sixth sense; they register the slight in their burgeoning psyches and serve it up later at various grown-up smorgasbords. Tonight would be one of those smorgasbords, with Amanda deciding which delight to serve up first. Maggie cringed at the thought.


It was the middle of dinner when Josephine's soup spoon abruptly hit the side of the china bowl making a clinking noise. Amanda smiled; Maggie blanched.

"You're a what?" Josephine asked, wiping what appeared to be perspiration from her upper lip.

"She's a lesbian, Gram, as in sleeps with women."

"But you are, were, a happily married woman. You're a mother and you're middle-aged. How can you be one of those?"

"A lesbian. It's not unheard of. I did intend to tell you in a more subtle way," Maggie said, pursing her lips and cocking her head in Amanda's direction. "It just happened and now I plan to deal with whatever changing one's sexuality entails, aside from therapy."

Josephine closed her mouth. She had been about to suggest that.

"I don't understand. Wouldn't you have had some sign of those feelings toward women sooner?"

"I probably did. I just didn't know what they were. After this all happened, lots of loose ends started to make sense to me. Mother, I've never felt this whole or happy before now."

"You've been brainwashed. Down there hanging out with all those funky women, a cult of lesbos in the middle of the desert. I'm sure if you stayed here you'd change your mind and give up this insanity," Amanda screeched.

"No, I wouldn't. I'm going out for coffee tomorrow morning with a lesbian I met today at the bookstore. Even if I wasn't in Arizona, I would still be a lesbian."

"So you're not just thinking about this. You've actually slept with a woman," Josephine said tentatively.

"Two to be exact."

Maggie hadn't intended that much shock value, but she had hit hard. She could read it in her mother's face. She had hoped that her being an adult would make this easier on her mother. She could see it was not going to be as simple as she would have liked.

Her mother attempted another tactic. "Are you sure that you're not still suffering some of the aftershocks of Harold's death? I can understand how you might feel safe and protected, even loved and nurtured, in a more feminine environment, but that doesn't mean you are necessarily like that."

"No, Mother, I am definitely like that. I've always loved Celia, and if I'd known what to do about it twenty years ago I wouldn't have married Harold."

"And then you wouldn't be burdened with me," Amanda shrieked, running from the room.

Maggie buried her face in her hands. "I shouldn't have said it like that. I didn't mean it like that."

Maggie heard her mother's chair as it scraped across the floor. She expected her to go after Amanda, to stroke the child's broken wing. Instead, Maggie felt her soft touch on her own shoulders. Her mother sat in the chair next to her and took her hands. She looked deep into Maggie's eyes and wiped away the one tear that ran down her cheek.

"You've had a tough time of it. Harold was not the one great love of your life, and that always bothered me. It must have been hard to be needed so desperately by two people who were selfish and not to have enough passion to fill up all that Harold and Amanda took from you. I always respected your strength and determination. I know that you did your best. The rest of your life should be spent loving

whom you want and living where you want. I may
not join PFLAG, but I certainly hope I get invited
for a visit. I always did like Celia."

Maggie smiled. "Thanks, Mom."

Maggie drove home that evening thinking that the
old lady had grace and enough wisdom to know when
to give in. Her mother would be a powerful ally. If
anyone could get Amanda to come around, she could.


PFLAG. How did she know about that? Maggie
wondered. Am I the only one who lived in a
homosexual mecca and didn't even think about it? I
must have been living in a cloud. She sipped her
coffee and smiled at Sam who smiled back.

"Thinking about last night?" Sam asked.

"Is it that obvious?" Maggie asked.

"It is a big deal. Coming out is never easy."

"Did I do a good job?"

"Anything short of denial is a good job."

"What did your mother think about all of it?"

"She wasn't exactly thrilled. But what the fuck.
They get used to things. She's better now. Everyone
gets through somehow or another. She knows I'm
happy, and that counts for a lot. She doesn't brag
about me at the office, but that's okay. What do I
care? I'm me and I know who I am, and that's
important. Anything else is extraneous bullshit."

"I wish I had your confidence," said Maggie. She
was wistful, thinking back to being young and
knowing what your expectations are, not being
wishy-washy and simply making choices by absentee
ballot. No wonder Amanda hated her.

Maggie didn't see how she could straighten up

and become a real parent. It was too late for that. Her father had tried it, deciding to become a parent when it was too late. Maggie had let go of him a long time before, and try as he might, he couldn't reel her back in. Now she realized she had done the same thing to her own child.

"I think I found the perfect realtor for you. Her name is Lucretia Freeman, foremost dyke realtor. She deals in big properties like I'm sure your house is."

"What makes you so certain of that?"

"The car is a dead giveaway," Sam said, cocking her head in the direction of the BMW.

"I guess it is a good-size house."

"Why are you so apathetic toward your possessions? Don't tell me you're one of those rich women who have everything and are still miserable. I'd shit for a car like that."

"Not if you were pretending to be something you know you're not."

"Like what?"

"Like an overeducated, underachieving doctor's wife who is really a closet lesbian."

"So where's doc now?"

"He died last year."

"I'm sorry."

"Don't be. He lived a good life, got most of what he wanted — except, maybe, a truly devoted wife, but that was partly his own fault. That's what happens when you compromise."

"What was the compromise?"

"My best friend and his fiancée ran off with another woman."

"So you two hooked up out of pain and loneliness."

161

"Precisely."

"How did you hook up with your ladylove in Arizona?"

"She's the best friend and fiancée."

"You're shitting."

"Small world. We finished what never got started."

"Does it feel right?"

"Very."

"Then that's all that matters."


Maggie went home wondering if Sam was the incarnation of her guardian angel, showing up at just the right time to keep things going. Maggie had felt herself slowing down, becoming inert. She didn't know why or how, but she could feel it.

Then Maggie had the dream. She dreamed that she saw Celia and they made love, and then Maggie said I can't believe I don't wake up next to you each morning. In the dream she felt the pain of having known love and having lost it.

Then there was Amanda, who wouldn't return her phone calls or answer the door when Maggie went to see her. It was getting so messy. But she had a realtor.


Maggie wasn't prepared for Lucretia when she cruised into the house. She was the embodiment of panache, dressed in an orange suit with short hair colored blonde and lipstick that seemed about to take over her face. She poked and prodded about the house.

"Do you care who buys the house?"

"What do you mean?"

"Honey, do you want straights or family?"

"Does it matter?"

"To some people it does. Most of my clients are family, but then Sam says you are, too," Lucretia said, raising an eyebrow and checking Maggie out as if she wasn't sure. "She says you're selling and running off to live with your lover somewhere in the southwest."

"Arizona."

"Yes, that's right. Is time a concern?"

"Yes. I want out as quickly as possible."

"Have you decided what's going and what's staying?"

"Not exactly. But I'll get on it," Maggie said, thinking that she hadn't even started cleaning out Harold's possessions. Messy. Things were so messy. How did she think she could run a business when she couldn't get around to selling the house?

After Lucretia left, Maggie called Celia.

Celia laughed hysterically at Maggie's description of the dyke realtor, but she could sense underneath Maggie's facade of humor that something was wrong, very wrong.

"Mag, what's going on?"

"Nothing. Everything is fine."

"Stop it. Tell me what's wrong. What are you feeling?"

"Oh, Celia. I'm a mess. I feel like I've got

163

concrete blocks tied to my limbs. I can't get myself to do anything. Amanda won't speak to me. I still haven't done anything with Harold's stuff. Lucretia wants to know what comes with the house. I don't even know what to keep, what to throw away."

"Get a piece of paper, and we'll make a to-do list."

"All right."

Together they made up a schedule. Maggie felt better when they were done.

When Celia got off the phone, she called everyone together.

"What's up?" Olivia asked.

"Maggie's not doing well. She needs some help."

"I knew it. We never should have let her go like that," Olivia said.

"Do you two think you could hold down the fort?" Celia asked Madeline and Kate.

"Of course."

"No problem."

Celia knew she couldn't leave Olivia behind, and she needed Anna to keep Olivia under control. She knew Olivia was fiercely attached to Maggie. She was more of a daughter than Amanda could ever hope to be.

"I need you two to come with me. Maggie needs some reinforcements. I was wrong to think she could tackle this by herself. I'll call for tickets. We'll leave as soon as I can get us a flight."

"Thank god. Let's get this shit cleared up and move on," Olivia said, getting up.

"Where are you going?" asked Celia.

"To pack."

"No time like the present," Anna said, getting up to follow her.

"At least I don't have to convince anyone," said Celia.

Olivia turned to look at her. "How could you have possibly thought she could do this by herself?"

"Olivia!" Anna said.

"Well, it's true. You let her clean up your mess the first time, and now you're letting her do it again. Isn't once enough?"

"You're right. I should have gone with her. I was being selfish."

"Damn straight!" said Olivia.

"Olivia, that's enough. We all have our own reasons for what we do, of which other people are not always aware. Now apologize and then go pack," Anna told her.

Olivia stared at both of them, momentarily stunned. "I'm sorry."

She turned and left.

"What was that?" asked Celia.

"I'd wager it was a prime example of tapping into the universal consciousness. For a moment Liv tapped into your experience, realized it, and was then released," Madeline explained.

"Oh," Celia replied, crinkling her brow.

"Personally, I think she realized she was being a crass asshole. Anyway, I'm glad we're hopping on our white steeds to rescue a damsel in distress. Maggie's not going to be upset that we came?" asked Anna.

"It's not like we don't have faith in her."

"She knows she needs help. There's no shame in that."

"Are you going to tell her we're coming?"

"No."

"Why not?"

"I don't know. I'm just not. Maybe I'm afraid she'll talk me out of it."

"Could she?"

"She did it once."

"Have you been back there at all in twenty years?"

"No, I haven't. It was a real disaster, lots of hurt feelings. Until now, there was no reason to go back."

"Do you think it will be any better this time?"

"I doubt it."

# Chapter Nine

Maggie sat in the middle of the den packing. She'd decided that she would start with Harold's stuff. If she could remove his presence from the house, she could tackle the rest more easily. Lucretia had given her a week before she would start showing the house.

She carefully wrapped newspaper around breakable items, even though she wasn't sure what she was going to do with them. She didn't want them. Maggie didn't want anything. She wondered at her lack of attachments to possessions. Maybe Sam was right.

She would ask Amanda if she wanted them — if Amanda ever spoke to her again.

Clearing up a life wasn't easy. It was as if both occupants of the house had died.

She poured herself another glass of wine. There was something to be said for fine wines, and she was drinking her way though Harold's wine collection.

Amanda appeared in the doorway of the den. She, too, had been drinking.

"What are you doing?"

"Packing," replied Maggie.

Amanda's face was flushed. Maggie felt her own color rising.

"So this is really it. You're doing it. Leaving us all in the wake of your disaster. You're a fucking deserter. Can't handle it, can you? I don't suppose it matters anyway. You never liked your life. You never loved us. You thought you fooled us, but you didn't. We knew."

"Amanda, that's not true."

"Yes, it is. Why don't you just torch the place? Why bother with all this care?" said Amanda, whisking the neat stack of newspaper off the table, the leaves flying about the room.

"Sit down. Let's talk," Maggie said, standing up.

"What is there to talk about? You've decided everything already. Leave and forget. Forget any of this ever happened. You're such a fucking coward."

"Amanda, stop it. I'm not going to stand here and listen to you abuse me. I love you, dammit. I have always loved you. I wasn't perfect. I never tried to be. I gave you the best I had. I'm sorry if that wasn't good enough. But I'm not going to stay here in order to make you happy. I deserve more than that."

"Oh, yes, you deserve everything. You deserve to be crushed into small pieces for being such a fake. For faking everything you were. I hate you. I hate this house, all these things, stupid things, things that are supposed to mean something, things that mean nothing." She picked up the nearest thing, a lamp, and pitched it against the wall dangerously close to Maggie's head. Maggie ducked.

"That's enough. This is my house, and I won't let you destroy it."

"Why not? You don't care about it," Amanda replied, grabbing something else to fling across the room. Maggie crouched down and covered her head, listening to the crash as it hit the wall. Amanda screamed at her. Books and crystal crashed around her and finally the chair flew through the window. Amanda was ripping the room apart, piece by piece, while Maggie cowered behind a stack of boxes. For a brief moment Maggie thought about calling the police, but Amanda ripped the phone from the wall and pitched it across the room. The bell chinged as it struck a hard surface.

Amanda's temper frightened her. She ran statistics through her head about instances of domestic violence perpetrated by a loved one. Suddenly — the crashes stopped, and she heard other voices.

"Jesus fucking Christ!"

It was Olivia's voice. Maggie thought she was hallucinating. Wishing for a savior, one had appeared.

Celia, Anna, and Olivia had been standing on the porch, suitcases in hand, when the desk chair went sailing through the window. Politeness was thrown to the wind as they barreled in the front door and stared at the madwoman who was throwing everything she could get her hands on across the room.

Olivia and Anna grabbed Amanda, restraining any more violence. Maggie looked up and saw Celia. Amanda was dragged off, struggling and screaming obscenities.

"Maybe the fresh air will clear her out," Olivia said as she helped carry Amanda out the kitchen door to the backyard.

"Nice house, hey," Anna said as they scurried past rooms.

"You fucking bitch!" Amanda screamed.

"Hey, that's enough of that. Your mother may not defend herself, but that doesn't stop me from knocking you flat," Olivia told her. "Now you can either sit in that chair nicely or I'll tie your ass to it. You need to calm down."

"Or we'll be forced to sit on you until you do. Now you wouldn't like that, would you? It's not very dignified," said Anna.

"You're so diplomatic," Olivia complimented her.

"Why, thank you."

"You two are the fucking nutcases," Amanda snarled.

"I didn't see either one of us pitching shit across the room at your mother. Did you?" Olivia asked, looking at Anna.

"No, as a matter of fact I didn't. Of course,

demolishing a den is not always a sign of insanity," replied Anna.

"Well, it certainly isn't a sign of stable mental health."

"I'm not going to sit here and listen to this shit," said Amanda, getting up. Olivia slammed her back into the chair.

"I don't think so, little lady. You're not going anywhere until we think you're ready."

"She should probably have to clean up the mess," said Anna.

"At the very least."

"I'm not some four-year-old that can be made to do things," said Amanda.

"Maybe you should stop acting like one. Besides, cleanup is probably preferable to being charged with aggravated assault."

"Maybe we should call the police now."

"I certainly hope you didn't hit your mother with any of those objects, because then we would be forced to take some drastic action," Anna said, narrowing her eyes at Amanda.

"I didn't hit her. I don't think I hit her," Amanda replied, beginning to come to her senses, trying to remember what she had done in her rage. Remorse crept in.


"Maggie, are you all right?" Celia asked, walking across the debris to where Maggie crouched.

Maggie got up and dusted herself off. "Would you like a glass of wine? I think I really need one." She looked around for a glass. There wasn't an intact one around. "Swig maybe," Maggie replied, taking one and handing the bottle to Celia.

"Timely arrival," said Maggie, drawing Celia to her and holding her. Celia could feel her shaking.

"Maggie, are you okay? She didn't hurt you, did she?"

"Celia," said Maggie, wiping the tears from her eyes but still smiling. "I'm so glad you're here. I can't do this on my own. I thought I was strong enough, but I'm not. You're not disappointed in me, are you?"

"No, not at all."

"What's your big problem? Surely you're not a mama's girl. Why clutch and grab at her when she would willingly hold you if you asked?" said Olivia.

"I shouldn't have to ask."

"Your mother is supposed to be telepathic on top of everything else?" Anna said, staring at Amanda. "What do you want from her? What sort of ultimate sacrifice do you expect?"

Amanda looked down at her hands. She honestly didn't know.

"I don't want her to be a lesbian."

"I think that fits in the category of an ultimate sacrifice. What do you think, Anna?"

"Yes, I think asking someone to give up how she feels, who she loves, and the chance to live a life she feels is right is definitely asking quite a bit. Tell me, have you always been this homophobic or is this something new?"

Amanda scowled at her.

"Maybe she is afraid her mother will turn into a diesel dyke and lose all her feminine qualities. She'll be embarrassed and forced to lie about her mother's whereabouts — or worse, pretend she's an orphan in case she meets the right man and he's just as homophobic as she is," said Olivia.

"I don't have to sit here and listen to this crap. All I know is that my mother was normal until she hooked up with you fucking perverts," Amanda said, getting up.

"Remember Amanda, perverted is a relative term. Don't think that walking out on your mother is going to make her come back."

"We'll see," Amanda said, walking away.


Celia looked over at Maggie as they walked along the river.

"Do you remember when I was leaving with Bridgette and you kissed me?"

Maggie looked at her and smiled. "Of course. That was my clue that maybe something wasn't quite right."

"I always wondered if you felt anything."

"I knew I was losing more than a friend."

"When you kissed me, I had a sudden insight that maybe I'd fallen in love with the wrong woman."

"And who was the right one?"

"You, silly. Come here," Celia said, pulling Maggie to her.

"I forgot what it was like to kiss with a cold nose."

"Me, too."



Olivia and Anna were making breakfast. Anna looked up from where she was chopping onions and potatoes. Amanda was halfway up the stairs before either one of them had a chance to move.

"Amanda, wait!" Olivia said, standing at the bottom of the stairs.

"I just want to talk to her," Amanda said calmly. "I won't do anything."

"Amanda, let me get them. Come down and have some coffee."

"No, I want to talk to her right now," Amanda said, walking down the hall.

Olivia looked at Anna and bit her lip.

"I hope they're just sleeping late."

"Me, too."

"Why do I get the feeling something awful is going to happen?" said Olivia.

"Because there is a pretty good chance that something could. Let's be positive. Celia is taking a shower and Maggie is sitting propped up in bed looking virginal and reading the paper."

"God, I hope you're right."

* * * * *

Maggie was rocking gently on top of Celia. She collapsed in delight. She looked over and saw Amanda staring at them with tears running down her face.

"Christ!" said Maggie, rolling off. Celia sat up to see Amanda dashing from the room.

"Amanda! Wait," Maggie said, wrapping a sheet around her and scrambling after her daughter. But it was too late. When she got back, Celia was getting dressed.

"Maggie, I'm so sorry."

"Amanda always did have a wretched sense of timing."

Olivia and Anna watched as Amanda went screaming past. They looked at each other.

"They were fucking," Olivia said, her voice flat.

"Good guess."

Celia came down first. They both looked up, feeling guilty.

"We tried to stop her," Olivia said.

"It's not your fault."

"Did she see anything?" Anna asked tentatively.

"A lot more than she should have."

"How's Maggie?"

"I don't know. She's taking a shower."

Maggie came down dressed and looking calm. She smiled at them. They watched her as she pulled a bottle of tequila from the cupboard above the sink. She poured herself a shot and downed it quickly.

"Well, I guess I won't be getting any more mushy Mother's Day cards," said Maggie. She burst into tears.

\* \* \* \* \*

That night as they lay in bed, Celia thought about the afternoon Harold found her in bed with Bridgette. Now his daughter had seen very much the same thing. The circular nature of life was beginning to disturb her. She had left this place twenty years ago, vowing not to return. It had been too painful. People that she loved and trusted turned on her in rapid succession. She felt like the lone survivor of a firing squad, wounded and left for dead.

Later, Celia awoke to find Maggie crying in the night. They didn't speak. They held each other, and together they cried. They both knew that like Harold, Amanda would hold a lifelong grudge.

# Chapter Ten

Maggie and Celia sat on the Navajo rug in the middle of the now-empty living room. Nothing was left in the house but a mattress upstairs and the rug upon which they were sitting. They were having a picnic. It was cold outside, and the leaves had dropped from most of the trees. But sunlight poured in the large front window, and rainbow splashes of light from the lead glass panes danced across the floor.

"Thinking about the house?"

"How'd you guess?"

"I could see it in your eyes. Will you miss it?"

"No. I have a new home now."

"Good."

Maggie's mother took them to the airport. Olivia and Anna had left early, eager to get back to work and get away from the bleakness of oncoming winter. They had all stayed longer than was intended, and each was grateful to be going home.

"Well, darling, you got your wish, and I'm glad."

Maggie took her mother's hand.

"Why can't Amanda be more like you and less like Harold?"

"Stubbornness will forever find a foothold. It dies off in one place and crops up in another. She might come around someday. I'll keep an eye on her. Give her time. She'll miss you, and then she'll learn to overlook what she can't agree with."

"I hope you're right."

"Well, ladies, off you go. I'll try to be down in February when I'm thoroughly sick of winter and need some respite. Celia, take care," said Josephine.

She gave them both a hug. Maggie felt her eyes moisten. The attendant took their tickets. Maggie looked back to see her mother walking away. Celia took her hand, and they boarded the plane.

Olivia and Anna met them at the gate when they landed. It was good to be back. Good to have Celia's hand on her thigh. Good to have Olivia and Anna cheerfully bantering as they drove back to the ranch.


Maggie stood on the porch listening to the wind as it rustled softly through the palms. The sun slowly dove into the sea of sand, and she heard the others making preparations for dinner, the clanking of plates and glasses, the friendly chatter, the pop as the cork was pulled from the bottle of wine. Celia cracked the door, sticking her head through it and smiling.

"Dinner's ready."

"I'll be right there," Maggie said, sighing. I'm home, I'm finally home, she thought as she walked through the door, taking one last look behind her.

A few of the publications of
**THE NAIAD PRESS, INC.**
P.O. Box 10543 • Tallahassee, Florida 32302
Phone (904) 539-5965
Toll-Free Order Number: 1-800-533-1973
*Mail orders welcome. Please include 15% postage.*
*Write or call for our free catalog which also features an*
*incredible selection of lesbian videos.*

THE SEARCH by Melanie McAllester. 240 pp. Exciting top cop
Tenny Mendoza case.                           ISBN 1-56280-150-3    $10.95

THE WISH LIST by Saxon Bennett. 192 pp. Romance through
the years.                                    ISBN 1-56280-125-2     10.95

FIRST IMPRESSIONS by Kate Calloway. 208 pp. P.I. Cassidy
James' first case.                            ISBN 1-56280-133-3     10.95

OUT OF THE NIGHT by Kris Bruyer. 192 pp. Spine-tingling
thriller.                                     ISBN 1-56280-120-1     10.95

NORTHERN BLUE by Tracey Richardson. 224 pp. Police recruits
Miki & Miranda — passion in the line of fire.  ISBN 1-56280-118-X    10.95

LOVE'S HARVEST by Peggy Herring. 176 pp. by the author of
*Once More With Feeling.*                      ISBN 1-56280-117-1     10.95

THE COLOR OF WINTER by Lisa Shapiro. 208 pp. Romantic
love beyond your wildest dreams.              ISBN 1-56280-116-3     10.95

FAMILY SECRETS by Laura DeHart Young. 208 pp. Enthralling
romance and suspense.                         ISBN 1-56280-119-8     10.95

INLAND PASSAGE by Jane Rule. 288 pp. Tales exploring conven-
tional & unconventional relationships.        ISBN 0-930044-56-8     10.95

DOUBLE BLUFF by Claire McNab. 208 pp. 7th Detective Carol
Ashton Mystery.                               ISBN 1-56280-096-5     10.95

BAR GIRLS by Lauran Hoffman. 176 pp. See the movie, read
the book!                                     ISBN 1-56280-115-5     10.95

THE FIRST TIME EVER edited by Barbara Grier & Christine
Cassidy. 272 pp. Love stories by Naiad Press authors.
                                              ISBN 1-56280-086-8     14.95

MISS PETTIBONE AND MISS McGRAW by Brenda Weathers.
208 pp. A charming ghostly love story.        ISBN 1-56280-151-1     10.95

CHANGES by Jackie Calhoun. 208 pp. Involved romance and
relationships.                                ISBN 1-56280-083-3     10.95

FAIR PLAY by Rose Beecham. 256 pp. 3rd Amanda Valentine
Mystery.                                    ISBN 1-56280-081-7    10.95

PAXTON COURT by Diane Salvatore. 256 pp. Erotic and wickedly
funny contemporary tale about the business of learning to live
together.                                   ISBN 1-56280-109-0    21.95

PAYBACK by Celia Cohen. 176 pp. A gripping thriller of romance,
revenge and betrayal.                       ISBN 1-56280-084-1    10.95

THE BEACH AFFAIR by Barbara Johnson. 224 pp. Sizzling
summer romance/mystery/intrigue.            ISBN 1-56280-090-6    10.95

GETTING THERE by Robbi Sommers. 192 pp. Nobody does it
like Robbi!                                 ISBN 1-56280-099-X    10.95

FINAL CUT by Lisa Haddock. 208 pp. 2nd Carmen Ramirez
Mystery.                                    ISBN 1-56280-088-4    10.95

FLASHPOINT by Katherine V. Forrest. 256 pp. A Lesbian
blockbuster!                                ISBN 1-56280-079-5    10.95

CLAIRE OF THE MOON by Nicole Conn. Audio Book —Read
by Marianne Hyatt.                          ISBN 1-56280-113-9    16.95

FOR LOVE AND FOR LIFE: INTIMATE PORTRAITS OF
LESBIAN COUPLES by Susan Johnson. 224 pp.
                                            ISBN 1-56280-091-4    14.95

DEVOTION by Mindy Kaplan. 192 pp. See the movie — read
the book!                                   ISBN 1-56280-093-0    10.95

SOMEONE TO WATCH by Jaye Maiman. 272 pp. 4th Robin
Miller Mystery.                             ISBN 1-56280-095-7    10.95

GREENER THAN GRASS by Jennifer Fulton. 208 pp. A young
woman — a stranger in her bed.              ISBN 1-56280-092-2    10.95

TRAVELS WITH DIANA HUNTER by Regine Sands. Erotic
lesbian romp. Audio Book (2 cassettes)      ISBN 1-56280-107-4    16.95

CABIN FEVER by Carol Schmidt. 256 pp. Sizzling suspense
and passion.                                ISBN 1-56280-089-1    10.95

THERE WILL BE NO GOODBYES by Laura DeHart Young. 192
pp. Romantic love, strength, and friendship.    ISBN 1-56280-103-1    10.95

FAULTLINE by Sheila Ortiz Taylor. 144 pp. Joyous comic
lesbian novel.                              ISBN 1-56280-108-2     9.95

OPEN HOUSE by Pat Welch. 176 pp. 4th Helen Black Mystery.
                                            ISBN 1-56280-102-3    10.95

ONCE MORE WITH FEELING by Peggy J. Herring. 240 pp.
Lighthearted, loving romantic adventure.    ISBN 1-56280-089-2    10.95

FOREVER by Evelyn Kennedy. 224 pp. Passionate romance — love
overcoming all obstacles.                   ISBN 1-56280-094-9    10.95

WHISPERS by Kris Bruyer. 176 pp. Romantic ghost story
                                            ISBN 1-56280-082-5    10.95

NIGHT SONGS by Penny Mickelbury. 224 pp. 2nd Gianna Maglione
Mystery.                                    ISBN 1-56280-097-3    10.95

GETTING TO THE POINT by Teresa Stores. 256 pp. Classic
southern Lesbian novel.                     ISBN 1-56280-100-7    10.95

PAINTED MOON by Karin Kallmaker. 224 pp. Delicious
Kallmaker romance.                          ISBN 1-56280-075-2    10.95

THE MYSTERIOUS NAIAD edited by Katherine V. Forrest &
Barbara Grier. 320 pp. Love stories by Naiad Press authors.
                                            ISBN 1-56280-074-4    14.95

DAUGHTERS OF A CORAL DAWN by Katherine V. Forrest.
240 pp. Tenth Anniversay Edition.           ISBN 1-56280-104-X    10.95

BODY GUARD by Claire McNab. 208 pp. 6th Carol Ashton
Mystery.                                    ISBN 1-56280-073-6    10.95

CACTUS LOVE by Lee Lynch. 192 pp. Stories by the beloved
storyteller.                                ISBN 1-56280-071-X     9.95

SECOND GUESS by Rose Beecham. 216 pp. 2nd Amanda Valentine
Mystery.                                    ISBN 1-56280-069-8     9.95

THE SURE THING by Melissa Hartman. 208 pp. L.A. earthquake
romance.                                    ISBN 1-56280-078-7     9.95

A RAGE OF MAIDENS by Lauren Wright Douglas. 240 pp. 6th Caitlin
Reece Mystery.                              ISBN 1-56280-068-X    10.95

TRIPLE EXPOSURE by Jackie Calhoun. 224 pp. Romantic drama
involving many characters.                  ISBN 1-56280-067-1     9.95

UP, UP AND AWAY by Catherine Ennis. 192 pp. Delightful
romance.                                    ISBN 1-56280-065-5     9.95

PERSONAL ADS by Robbi Sommers. 176 pp. Sizzling short
stories.                                    ISBN 1-56280-059-0     9.95

FLASHPOINT by Katherine V. Forrest. 256 pp. Lesbian
blockbuster!                                ISBN 1-56280-043-4    22.95

CROSSWORDS by Penny Sumner. 256 pp. 2nd Victoria Cross
Mystery.                                    ISBN 1-56280-064-7     9.95

SWEET CHERRY WINE by Carol Schmidt. 224 pp. A novel of
suspense.                                   ISBN 1-56280-063-9     9.95

CERTAIN SMILES by Dorothy Tell. 160 pp. Erotic short stories.
                                            ISBN 1-56280-066-3     9.95

EDITED OUT by Lisa Haddock. 224 pp. 1st Carmen Ramirez
Mystery.                                    ISBN 1-56280-077-9     9.95

WEDNESDAY NIGHTS by Camarin Grae. 288 pp. Sexy
adventure.                                  ISBN 1-56280-060-4    10.95

SMOKEY O by Celia Cohen. 176 pp. Relationships on the
playing field.                              ISBN 1-56280-057-4     9.95

KATHLEEN O'DONALD by Penny Hayes. 256 pp. Rose and
Kathleen find each other and employment in 1909 NYC.
                                    ISBN 1-56280-070-1        9.95

STAYING HOME by Elisabeth Nonas. 256 pp. Molly and Alix
want a baby . . . or do they?       ISBN 1-56280-076-0       10.95

TRUE LOVE by Jennifer Fulton. 240 pp. Six lesbians searching
for love in all the "right" places.   ISBN 1-56280-035-3      10.95

GARDENIAS WHERE THERE ARE NONE by Molleen Zanger.
176 pp. Why is Melanie inextricably drawn to the old house?
                                    ISBN 1-56280-056-6        9.95

KEEPING SECRETS by Penny Mickelbury. 208 pp. 1st Gianna
Maglione Mystery.                   ISBN 1-56280-052-3        9.95

THE ROMANTIC NAIAD edited by Katherine V. Forrest &
Barbara Grier. 336 pp. Love stories by Naiad Press authors.
                                    ISBN 1-56280-054-X       14.95

UNDER MY SKIN by Jaye Maiman. 336 pp. 3rd Robin Miller
Mystery.                            ISBN 1-56280-049-3.      10.95

STAY TOONED by Rhonda Dicksion. 144 pp. Cartoons — 1st
collection since *Lesbian Survival Manual.*    ISBN 1-56280-045-0      9.95

CAR POOL by Karin Kallmaker. 272pp. Lesbians on wheels
and then some!                      ISBN 1-56280-048-5       10.95

NOT TELLING MOTHER: STORIES FROM A LIFE by Diane
Salvatore. 176 pp. Her 3rd novel.   ISBN 1-56280-044-2        9.95

GOBLIN MARKET by Lauren Wright Douglas. 240pp. 5th Caitlin
Reece Mystery.                      ISBN 1-56280-047-7       10.95

LONG GOODBYES by Nikki Baker. 256 pp. 3rd Virginia Kelly
Mystery.                            ISBN 1-56280-042-6        9.95

FRIENDS AND LOVERS by Jackie Calhoun. 224 pp. Midwestern Lesbian lives and loves.    ISBN 1-56280-041-8       10.95

THE CAT CAME BACK by Hilary Mullins. 208 pp. Highly
praised Lesbian novel.              ISBN 1-56280-040-X        9.95

BEHIND CLOSED DOORS by Robbi Sommers. 192 pp. Hot,
erotic short stories.               ISBN 1-56280-039-6        9.95

CLAIRE OF THE MOON by Nicole Conn. 192 pp. See the
movie — read the book!              ISBN 1-56280-038-8       10.95

SILENT HEART by Claire McNab. 192 pp. Exotic Lesbian
romance.                            ISBN 1-56280-036-1       10.95

HAPPY ENDINGS by Kate Brandt. 272 pp. Intimate conversations
with Lesbian authors.               ISBN 1-56280-050-7       10.95

THE SPY IN QUESTION by Amanda Kyle Williams. 256 pp.
4th Madison McGuire Mystery.        ISBN 1-56280-037-X        9.95

SAVING GRACE by Jennifer Fulton. 240 pp. Adventure and
romantic entanglement. ISBN 1-56280-051-5    9.95

THE YEAR SEVEN by Molleen Zanger. 208 pp. Women surviving
in a new world. ISBN 1-56280-034-5    9.95

CURIOUS WINE by Katherine V. Forrest. 176 pp. Tenth Anniver-
sary Edition. The most popular contemporary Lesbian love story.
ISBN 1-56280-053-1    10.95
Audio Book (2 cassettes) ISBN 1-56280-105-8    16.95

CHAUTAUQUA by Catherine Ennis. 192 pp. Exciting, romantic
adventure. ISBN 1-56280-032-9    9.95

A PROPER BURIAL by Pat Welch. 192 pp. 3rd Helen Black
Mystery. ISBN 1-56280-033-7    9.95

SILVERLAKE HEAT: A Novel of Suspense by Carol Schmidt.
240 pp. Rhonda is as hot as Laney's dreams. ISBN 1-56280-031-0    9.95

LOVE, ZENA BETH by Diane Salvatore. 224 pp. The most talked
about lesbian novel of the nineties! ISBN 1-56280-030-2    10.95

A DOORYARD FULL OF FLOWERS by Isabel Miller. 160 pp.
Stories incl. 2 sequels to *Patience and Sarah*. ISBN 1-56280-029-9    9.95

MURDER BY TRADITION by Katherine V. Forrest. 288 pp. 4th
Kate Delafield Mystery. ISBN 1-56280-002-7    10.95

THE EROTIC NAIAD edited by Katherine V. Forrest & Barbara
Grier. 224 pp. Love stories by Naiad Press authors.
ISBN 1-56280-026-4    14.95

DEAD CERTAIN by Claire McNab. 224 pp. 5th Carol Ashton
Mystery. ISBN 1-56280-027-2    9.95

CRAZY FOR LOVING by Jaye Maiman. 320 pp. 2nd Robin Miller
Mystery. ISBN 1-56280-025-6    9.95

STONEHURST by Barbara Johnson. 176 pp. Passionate regency
romance. ISBN 1-56280-024-8    10.95

INTRODUCING AMANDA VALENTINE by Rose Beecham.
256 pp. 1st Amanda Valentine Mystery. ISBN 1-56280-021-3    9.95

UNCERTAIN COMPANIONS by Robbi Sommers. 204 pp.
Steamy, erotic novel. ISBN 1-56280-017-5    9.95

A TIGER'S HEART by Lauren W. Douglas. 240 pp. 4th·Caitlin
Reece Mystery. ISBN 1-56280-018-3    9.95

PAPERBACK ROMANCE by Karin Kallmaker. 256 pp. A
delicious romance. ISBN 1-56280-019-1    9.95

These are just a few of the many Naiad Press titles — we are the oldest and
largest lesbian/feminist publishing company in the world. Please request a
complete catalog. We offer personal service; we encourage and welcome
direct mail orders from individuals who have limited access to bookstores
carrying our publications.